PROMISE TO A DYING MAN

It was obviously costing the old man a lot to talk. "That last one Logan put inta me, just before they lit out. Hurt the worst. They was lousy shots, but he took his time with that one. They had the gold by then. I wanted 'em gone before you got back. Those treacherous bastards wouldn't think nothin' o' shootin' a boy. . . ."

Suddenly his whole body stiffened. Luther bent closer, talking, his voice hard. "I want you to hear this. You said they'd shoot a boy. Well, maybe I'm not such a boy anymore. I'm going after them. I'm going to run them down. I'm going to find them and kill them. For you."

The old man's eyes refocused on Luther's face. "By God, Luther, I think you might just do that."

DESPERADO

*   *   *

Special Preview!

Turn to the back of this book for an exciting excerpt from book two of the *Desperado* series, *EDGE OF THE LAW*

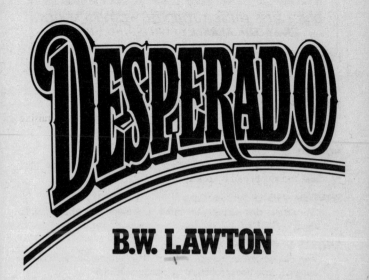

DESPERADO

B.W. LAWTON

JOVE BOOKS, NEW YORK

DESPERADO

A Jove Book / published by arrangement with
the author

PRINTING HISTORY
Jove edition / April 1993

All rights reserved.
Copyright © 1993 by Jove Publications, Inc.
This book may not be reproduced in whole
or in part, by mimeograph or any other means,
without permission. For information address:
The Berkley Publishing Group,
200 Madison Avenue,
New York, New York 10016

ISBN: 0-515-11077-9

Jove Books are published by The Berkley Publishing Group,
200 Madison Avenue, New York, New York 10016.
The name "JOVE" and the "J" logo
are trademarks belonging to Jove Publications, Inc.

PRINTED IN THE UNITED STATES OF AMERICA

10 9 8 7 6 5 4 3 2 1

CHAPTER ONE

The wolf loped through the brush, moving soundlessly over the sandy soil. From time to time it stopped, testing the air, scanning its surroundings, listening. It was an old wolf, had grown old because of its caution, because of listening, watching, never showing itself. There once had been many wolves in the area, but most were gone now, most dead, killed by men with rifles, and traps, and poison. This particular wolf had long ago learned to avoid man, or anything that smelled of man. And it had survived.

It was late spring; the sagebrush still showed some green. The wolf had been eating well lately; many animals browsed on that green, and the wolf browsed on the animals, the smaller ones, the ones he could catch by himself. There were no longer any wolf packs to pull down bigger game, deer, antelope. Life was now a succession of small meals, barely mouthfuls.

The wolf was thirsty. A quarter of a mile ahead a patch of thicker green showed. A water hole. The wolf could smell the water. It increased its pace, loping along, bouncing on still-springy legs, tongue lolling from its mouth, yellow eyes alert.

A thicket of willows some fifteen feet high, grew up on the far side of the water hole. The wolf gave them a cursory scan. It raised its nose, its main warning system, and could smell only water, willows, and mud.

It was late enough in the season for the water hole to have shrunk to a scummy puddle, no more than a foot deep and twenty feet across. In winter, when the rains came, the water formed a small lake. One more look around, then the wolf dropped its muzzle, pushed scum aside, and lapped slowly at the water.

1

After half a minute the wolf raised its head again, turning it from side to side, nervous. The water had claimed its attention for a dangerously long time.

Suddenly, the wolf froze. Perhaps the horse had made a small movement. Horses do not like the company of wolves, yet this one had stood motionless while the wolf approached, held so by the man on its back. The wolf saw him then, the man, blending into the willow thicket, mounted, sitting perfectly motionless.

A moment's stab of fear, the wolf's muscles bunching, ready to propel him away. But the wolf did not run. Ears pricked high, it stood still, looking straight at the man, sensing that he meant it no harm. Sensing, in its wolf's brain, an affinity with this particular man.

Wolf and man continued to look at one another for perhaps a half a minute. Then the wolf, with great dignity, turned, and loped away. Within seconds it had vanished into the brush.

The man did not move until he could no longer see the wolf. Then, with gentle pressure from his knees, he urged the horse out of the willows, down toward the water hole, where he let it drink again. The horse had been drinking earlier, head down, legs splayed out, when the man had first seen the wolf, or rather, seen movement, about a quarter of a mile away, a flicker of gray gliding through the chaparral. He was not quite sure why he'd backed his horse into the willows, why he'd quieted the animal down as the wolf approached. Perhaps he wanted to see if it could be done, if he could become invisible to the wolf. Because if he could do that, he should be able to become invisible to anything.

The wind had been from the wolf's direction. The horse's hooves had crushed some water plants at the edge of the pool; they gave off a strong odor, masking the man's scent, masking the horse's. A trick old Jedadiah had shown him, all those years ago . . . let nature herself conceal you.

He'd watched as the wolf approached the water hole, made one last quick check of its surroundings, then began to drink. A big, gaunt old fellow. The man wondered how the hell it had survived. Damned stockmen had done their best to exterminate every wolf within five hundred miles. Exterminate everything except their cows.

He was aware of the moment the wolf sensed his presence, knew it would happen an instant before it actually did. He watched the wolf's head rise, its body tense. But he knew that it would not

run. Or rather, sensed it. No, more than that . . . it was as if he and
the wolf shared a single mind, were the same species. Brothers.
The man smiled. Why not? Both he and the wolf shared a way
of life—they were both the hunter and the hunted.

The wolf was gone now, the moment over, and the man, pulling
his horse's head up from the water before it drank too much, left
the pool and rode out into the brush. And as he rode, anyone able
to watch from some celestial vantage point would have noticed
that he travelled pretty much as the wolf had travelled, almost
invisible in the brush, just flickers of movement as he guided his
horse over a route that would expose him the least, avoiding high
ground, never riding close to clumps of brush that were too thick
to see into, places that might conceal other men.

He rode until about an hour before dark, then he began to look
for a place to make camp for the night. He found it a quarter of an
hour later, a small depression surrounded by fairly thick chaparral,
but not so thick that he could not see out through it.

Dismounting, he quickly stripped the gear from his horse, the
bedroll and saddlebags coming off first, laid neatly together near
the place where he knew he would build a small fire. He drew his
two rifles, the big Sharps and the lighter Winchester, from their
saddle scabbards and propped them against a bush, within easy
reach. The saddle came off next; he heard his horse sigh with
relief when he loosened the girth.

Reaching into his saddlebags, the man pulled out a hackamore
made of soft, braided leather. Working with the ease that comes
from doing the same thing dozens of times, he slipped the bit
and bridle off his horse, and replaced it with the hackamore.
Now, the horse would be able to graze as it wished, without a
mouthful of iron bit in the way. More importantly, if there was
danger, if the man had to leave immediately, he would have some
kind of headstall already on his horse. When trouble came, speed
was essential. Thus the hackamore, and the style of his saddle, a
center-fire rig, less stable than a double rig, but easy to throw on
a horse when you were in a hurry.

The man fastened a long lead rope to the hackamore, tied the
free end to a stout bush, then left his horse free to move where
it wanted. He allowed himself a minute to sink down onto the
sandy ground, studying the area around him, alert, but also aware
of the peacefulness of the place. There was no sound at all except
the soft movement of the warm breeze through the bushes, and,
a hundred yards away, a single bird, singing its heart out.

In the midst of this quiet the man was aware of the workings of his mind. He was comfortable with his mind, liked to let it roam free, liked to watch the way it worked. He had learned over the years that most other men were uneasy with their minds, tried to blot them out with liquor, drugs, or religion.

His gaze wandered over to his horse. To the hackamore. He remembered the original Spanish word for halter—*jáquima*, altered now by the Anglo cowboy. Through his reading, and he read a great deal, the man had discovered that many of the words the Western horseman used were of Spanish origin, usually changed almost beyond recognition. When the first American cowboys came out West, they learned their trade from the original Western settlers, the Spanish vaqueros. Matchless horsemen, those Spaniards, especially out in California. God, they could ride!

When the Anglos moved into Texas, it was the local Mexicans who'd taught them how to handle cattle in those wide open spaces. Yet, he knew that most cowboys were totally unaware of the roots of the words they used every day. Not this man. He liked to think about words, about meanings, mysteries. He had an unquenchable hunger to learn.

And at the moment, a more basic hunger. There was movement off to his left; a jackrabbit, one of God's more stupid creatures, was hopping toward him. The rabbit stopped about ten yards away, then stood up on its hind legs so that it could more easily study this strange-smelling object. Rabbit and man were both immobile for several seconds, watching one another, then the man moved, one smooth motion, the pistol on his hip now in his hand, the hammer snicking back, the roar of a shot racketing around the little depression.

Peering through a big cloud of white gun smoke, the man thought at first he had missed; he could not see the rabbit. But then he did see it, or what was left of it, lying next to a bush a yard from where it had been sitting when he'd fired. He got up, went over to the dead rabbit. The big .45 caliber bullet had not left much of the head or front quarters, but that didn't matter. The hindquarters were where the meat was.

It took him less than five minutes to skin and gut the rabbit. He methodically picked out the big parasitic worms that lived beneath the rabbit's scruffy hide, careful not to smash them and ruin the meat. Ugly things. It took another fifteen minutes to get a fire going, and while the fire burned down to hot coals, the man whittled a spit out of a springy manzanita branch, and ran it through the rabbit.

It was dark before the rabbit was cooked. After seeing those worms, the man wanted to make sure the meat was done all the way through. He ate slowly, trying not to burn his fingers. For dessert he fished a small can of peaches out of his saddlebags. His only drink was warm, brackish water from his canteen. But he considered the meal a success, not so much because of the bill of fare, but because of the elegance of his surroundings: the pristine cleanness of the sandy ground on which he sat, the perfume of the chaparral, the broad band of the Milky Way arching overhead undimmed by man-made illumination.

Yeah, he thought, pretty damned beautiful. He scratched his chin through a week's unshaven bristle. And reflected that his life was damned lonely sometimes. Well, that was a choice he'd made, way back, and he was a man who stuck with his decisions.

Still, it could get damned lonely.

CHAPTER TWO

He woke up at first light, lying perfectly still for several seconds, then he turned his head slowly, to look over at the campsite, the place where he'd cooked and eaten the rabbit and left his horse and gear. As usual, he'd slept apart from his camp, so that anyone attempting to creep up on him during the night would try the wrong place.

Two books lay next to his bedroll. His Winchester lay across the books, to keep its working parts out of the sand. He moved the Winchester on top of the bedroll, then picked up one of the books, shifting position as the pistol inside the bedroll pressed against his side. He turned the book's pages to the place he had marked, and began to read. It was one of his favorite books; he chipped away at it whenever he had a little extra time. The writer was Thucydides; it was an account of the Peloponnesian Wars, the long struggle between Athens and Sparta. The immediacy of the text always amazed him. Although Thucydides had written the book nearly 2300 years ago, he might have been recounting today's events . . . politics, greed, war.

He read slowly, puzzling at the words. The copy he was reading was in Greek. He knew less than half the words. Exasperated, he picked up the other copy, which was in English, turned to the same section, and started comparing. For a while he became caught up in the English version, lost in the tale of an assault on a city. He forced himself back to the Greek version, determined to master it. He could already read Latin fairly well.

He slid out of his bedroll half an hour later. Since there was no water anywhere near, he had no way to wash, so he immediately broke camp. It took only a few minutes to saddle and bridle the horse, and pack his gear aboard. He swung up into the saddle, took a moment to check his surroundings from this greater height, then rode away from his one-night camp.

He rode all day, heading vaguely west, with no particular destination In mind, knowing only that mountains lay ahead. He liked mountains. Hell, he liked plains, too. Liked wild places in general.

He stopped at midday to chew on some jerky from his saddlebags, while his horse cropped the tough dry-land grass that grew in random clumps under bushes. Mounting again, he continued his journey. In the middle of the afternoon he saw movement ahead, the kind of movement made by men. He pulled his horse into a thick patch of brush and watched half a dozen riders pass by a quarter of a mile away. They were accompanying two big freight wagons. Pulling out a pair of binoculars, careful that sunlight did not reflect off the lenses, he studied the riders and the wagons. No one he knew, no one who might have an interest in him. Still, better to kind of sniff the air. Like that old wolf.

After the riders and wagons were out of sight, he continued on. He saw a town late in the afternoon, a smear of ratty construction at the foot of a range of hills. He sat his horse for a while, looking at the town. He decided to ride nearer. He rode far around to one side, coming at the town from the direction of the hills. Here, he had cover, and he used it as he approached. The light was beginning to go. Dismounting, he took out his binoculars and studied the town for several minutes. Not much of a place, one main street with a few alleys running off at more or less right angles. The usual rough wooden buildings, with the biggest ones facing the main street, and some houses—shacks, more or less— scattered haphazardly around the fringes.

One of the larger buildings, a long, low structure, looked a hell of a lot like a saloon. The man's throat, dry from the trail, gave an involuntary swallow. He started thinking about beer. A cool, foaming beer.

He studied the town one last time. There was hardly anyone in sight. None of the buildings looked like a jail, so there was probably no law around. Hell, he'd give it a try.

He waited until the last of the light was fading, then rode in, stopping his horse in the deep shade of a cottonwood tree, just short of the first buildings. After a few minutes of immobility, he decided there wasn't anything in the town worth worrying about.

He rode right up to the big building. It was a saloon all right, a little run-down looking, but definitely a saloon. That's what the warped sign over the front door said. He could just barely make out the lettering in the twilight. He stopped his horse at the hitching rack, dismounted, and tied the reins to the rack, careful to use a slipknot that would come free with one strong pull.

He looked around. Still no one in sight. He started toward the saloon's front door, then hesitated. Walking back to his horse, he slid the Winchester out of its scabbard, then opened the action far enough to made certain a shell was chambered. Satisfied, he stepped up onto the boardwalk, the rifle uncocked, but with his thumb near the hammer.

Inside the saloon, a faint buzz of boredom hummed through stagnant air. There was just one main room, with a bar running lengthwise along the left side. Tables were scattered over the rest of the splintery pine floor. A bartender stood behind the bar, which was quite long, mindlessly polishing a chipped glass, using a dirty cloth. A cowboy slumped against the bar, his right foot up on the sagging wooden rail. Further back in the room half a dozen men sat around two tables they'd pushed together, slowly knocking back cheap whiskey. Their mood was one of heavy boredom, as was the case most evenings in this particular wide spot in a very long road.

The swinging doors opened. Everyone looked up as a man pushed his way through. He was tall, wearing a big slouch hat, and carrying a Winchester. The moment the man was inside the room he slipped to one side, so that the wall was behind him. He stood for a moment, studying the room, then walked over to the bar, but with most of his body facing the part of the room where the half dozen men were seated. He ignored the cowboy. The man beckoned to the bartender. The barkeep gave the impression that he found this intrusion on his glass-polishing irritating, but he finally moved toward the stranger.

The stranger propped his rifle against the side of the bar. "You got any beer?" he asked. "Cold beer?"

The bartender shrugged. "Well, cold enough so's it won't boil eggs."

"I'll have one. With a whiskey chaser."

The bartender, turning ponderously, took down a beer mug— the stranger noticed approvingly that it was a large mug—and walked over to a big cask. It took him a couple of minutes to draw the beer; it foamed considerably. Walking back toward the stranger with the beer, foam slopping down the sides of the mug, he scooped up a bottle of whiskey on his way. The beer thudded down onto the bar top, spilling foam. The bottle followed, and the bartender was reaching for a shot glass when the stranger, having looked at the bottle, said, "No. Not that rotgut. I imagine you got something a little better tucked away somewhere."

The bartender turned back toward the man, prepared to be insulted, but he stopped dead, having for the first time looked the stranger directly in the face. Directly into a pair of the iciest eyes he'd ever seen. Cold blue eyes that were beginning to narrow down to slits. This is not a man to screw around with, a little voice deep inside the bartender's brain murmured. "Yessir," he said quickly. "Some real special stuff come in the other day. From back Tennessee way."

Another bottle thudded onto the bar top. The stranger picked it up, read the label, then nodded. The bartender hastily placed a glass on the bar top. The stranger filled his glass himself. After one more look around the room, a little like the way the wolf had looked around before lowering his head at the water hole, the man finally drank. First, a big draught of beer. His appreciative "Aaahhhh," could be heard all over the room. He picked up the shot glass and drank a little of the whiskey. After a few seconds he nodded his appreciation toward the bartender, who realized that he'd not been breathing much. The bartender let out a sigh of relief. The stranger's eyes, while still that same icy, unforgiving blue, were no longer narrowed down to slits.

There was a small stir of activity at the tables around which the half dozen men were seated. One of them, a man in his early twenties, chuckled. "Looka the way that there stranger's got Charlie hoppin'."

An older man, in his early forties, nodded. "Yeah. Buffaloed Charlie into givin' him some of our private stock."

Another man, older yet, pushing sixty, added his own nod. "Hard-looking feller. Don't think I'd wanna push him none."

All the men sat quietly for a while, studying the stranger. They saw a tall man, powerfully built, who moved with the grace and ease of a much lighter man. Thick chestnut hair showed beneath the rim of his hat. A drooping moustache of the same color screened a mouth that showed even, white teeth. He had a growth of trail beard several days old.

One of the men, Jack by name, the one who'd commented on the rape of their private-stock whiskey, the special-occasion brand, was studying more than the stranger's face. He noticed the pistol on his right hip, the way he wore it, low down, with a piece of rawhide tying the bottom of the holster to his leg. The top of the holster had been cut away, so that most of the revolver's trigger guard showed. A fighting man's rig.

Then, the man's clothing. A vest over a soft cotton shirt, and a short horseman's denim jacket over the vest. Nothing hanging low enough to interfere with the man's access to his pistol. Trousers looser than worn by the average brush popper. Trousers meant more for easy movement than for avoiding thorns. Not a cowboy's usual garb.

The boots. The lighting was not particularly strong, but, as the saying went, boots revealed the man. They were well-worn boots, but looked handmade. Looked as if they'd been molded to the man's feet. Expensive boots.

Jack took in more than just the man's clothing, dwelt, rather, on the entire picture. Nothing at all about the man shone or glittered or rattled. His spurs seemed to have been finagled in some way so that they did not jingle. Nor were there any fancy silver conchos decorating the spur straps. Nor jinglebobs dangling below the spurs, like some cowboys liked. Even the man's bandanna was a neutral color. There was nothing at all about him that would attract attention, lead one's eye toward him out on the trail.

A huge bowie knife hung from the man's belt, on the left, balancing the Colt on his right hip. The rifle he'd brought into the saloon with him was leaning against the bar next to his leg. A fighting man, Jack thought. And, from the way he came into the room, the way his back went right against the wall, maybe a man on the run.

Jack smiled. It had been a boring day. Hell, most days were boring in this godforsaken place. Maybe he could whip up a little activity. He turned toward the young man who'd spoken first, Davy. Jack didn't much like the kid, but he put up with him because Davy had a touchy temper, and the strength to make it carry. "That there fella," Jack said, nudging Davy. "Looks like one hard son of a bitch."

Davy, all youthful ego, as Jack well knew, immediately bridled. "Ah, he don't look all that tough to me. Ain't got the weight."

Weight, Jack mused. That's all the kid thinks about. His own beef. "Well," he drawled, "I know I wouldn't wanna mess with him."

Another of the men, having already figured out Jack's intention, added, straight-faced, trying not to grin, "Yeah, Davy. Not the kind o' man to mess with. He could tear a fella a new asshole."

"Ah, hell," Davy snorted disgustedly. "You all talk like a bunch o' little old ladies. As soon as a stranger comes in here. . . . Well, Gawd, just listen to you."

Several of the men grinned as Davy got to his feet, almost dumping his chair. The kid had been drinking quite a bit, and was just a little bit looped. Drunk enough to have soaked up a lot of liquid courage, but still sober enough to function. He headed toward the stranger.

Who saw him coming. Ah, shit, the man thought. There seems to be one in every town. He'd heard part of the conversation, knew what the other men were doing to the kid. A big kid, though. And packing a gun that rode high on his right hip, in a soft old holster that looked like the ass end of a sow.

Davy walked right up to the stranger. "Where you from, mister?" he asked, his manner not quite friendly, not quite hostile.

The stranger, whiskey glass in hand, looked the kid over for several seconds, long enough for Davy to start flushing with anger. "Around," the stranger finally said.

"Oh yeah?" Davy shot back, annoyed. "Cain't say I ever heard o' the place."

"It's small."

The stranger turned back to his drink. Davy waited a few seconds. "You got a name?"

The stranger turned back toward Davy. "So my mother told me."

Davy guffawed. "Hell. She probably didn't even know your father's name. I'll bet. . . ."

Davy's voice trailed off. Something had happened to the stranger's face. Before, it had reflected only boredom. But now . . .

The eyes. That was it . . . the change was in the eyes. They had narrowed down to two slits, half-hiding chips of blue ice. Surprisingly, the man's voice was soft when he finally spoke. "Kid. . . . Go away. Try and make it to your next birthday."

Davy didn't know what to say. Those eyes. . . . Then he heard someone from back at the table chuckling. Kind of a snicker, actually. Sounded like that prick, Jack. Davy flushed again. Anger was beginning to overcome his fear. "Why you . . ."

He reached out, to push the man's shoulder. Somehow he never connected. Whiskey splashed in his eyes, while at the same time something hooked his heel from behind. He felt a hand against his face, then he was falling. He hit hard, right on his tailbone. It hurt. He looked up. The man was looking disgustedly down at his empty whiskey glass. He put the glass down, picked up the bottle, poured more whiskey into the glass. The stranger didn't appear to be paying any attention to Davy at all. About the same attention he'd pay to a yapping puppy.

Which was more than Davy's machismo could take. He could hear soft laughter from back at the table, knew that the laughter was directed at him. His temper snapped; it was as if he was seeing everything through a bright red mist. "You son of a bitch!" he snarled, scrambling to stand up, his right hand reaching for his pistol.

No one in the room was able, later, to say just how it was done, how the stranger moved, but he simply took the pistol out of Davy's hand before the kid could even cock the hammer. The stranger turned the pistol around, pushed the muzzle against Davy's stomach. Davy froze. "I really don't want to kill you, kid," the stranger said. "But I will if you keep pushing it."

He did not say it loudly, but Davy had never heard such certainty in a man's voice. The stranger looked Davy straight in the eyes. Davy felt as If he were in a trap; he could not look away. He swallowed, tried to speak, but his throat was too dry.

The stranger took the gun muzzle out of Davy's belly, then threw the pistol away, skidding it along the bar. Six feet further along, it fell off, thumping loudly against the floor.

The bartender, afraid the pistol might break a bottle, had braced his hands below the bar, out of the stranger's sight. Relieved, he started to bring his right hand back up, turning toward the stranger. Once again, no one who saw it could quite describe just how it was done, but the stranger's pistol was suddenly in his right hand, pointed straight at the bartender's head, the hammer back. It was a move so fast, so smooth, that it had no separate components, just a single continuous flow.

The bartender froze, grinning a sickly grin as he showed the bar rag he was holding in his right hand. The stranger looked at him for a long second or two, then turned, and surveyed the room. Absolute stillness. No one was about to make the slightest move.

"This is a nervous-making place," the stranger said, sounding, for the first time, just a little pissed off. He smoothly slid his pistol back into its holster, then turned back toward the bar, picked up his glass, and took a sip of his whiskey. Davy was still just a few feet away, but he was afraid to move. Finally, the stranger looked at him over his shoulder, still obviously annoyed. Davy took it as a signal to leave, and started backing away. Backed all the way to the table. "Jesus God," he muttered as he collapsed into a chair.

Silence continued as the stranger finished his whiskey. Finally, he fished around in his pocket, pulled out fifty cents, and rang it down onto the bar. One last look around, then he picked up his rifle and headed toward the door. He didn't actually back out of the place—his exit was more dignified than that—but everyone was aware that he was watching the room all the way out the door, that they never actually saw his back.

Then he was gone. A collective sigh arose. "Jee-zuz!" one man murmured. "That was real close."

"Yeah," another man said, with a little more life. "Ain't seen nothin' like that since Wild Bill. . . ."

But now one of the older men was speaking, or rather, sputtering. "Hey! Hey! I . . . think I know that feller! Think I seen him before! Jesus Christ! Thought he was dead!"

"Well, hell," Jack cut in, having regained his former coolness. "Jesus Christ *is* dead, McGee. Ain't you heard? They strung him up, oh, hell, a long time ago."

"Uh-uh, Jack. None o' your funnin'. I say I know that feller."

Aware that everyone was hanging on his words, the old fellow built a dramatic pause. When he figured the tension was just right, he leaned a little forward and said, "That, gents, is the one they call the Desperado."

Silence. "Oh, Gawd," Davy muttered, white as a sheet. He suddenly turned toward Jack. "You son of a bitch!" he snapped. "You knew. You knew. You was tryin' to git me killed!"

But it was obvious that Jack was just as surprised as the others. "Well, I'll be damned," he murmured.

Another, shorter silence. "Guess he's as fast as they say," someone finally volunteered. "Hell, I heard about the time he—"

"Now wait just a damned minute," another man cut in. He'd only been out West a couple of years. "Just who the hell is this character, anyhow? Has he got a name?"

Which caused some head rubbing. "Well, you know," a man finally said, "I don't know if I ever heard he had a regular handle."

The old man, realizing he was losing the others' attention, said, "Hell, he don't *have* no regular name. An' you know why?"

Once again he tried to let a tense pause build, but, seeing that others were about to put in their two cents worth, he quickly said, " 'Cause he's a half-breed. White father, Shawnee mother. Never got himself no regular civilized name."

Another man shook his head in disgust. "You're talkin' through your asshole, McGee. All you gotta do is look at him an' you can see he ain't no half-breed. The way I heard it, he used to be a rancher out West Texas way. Doin' real well, until his wife an' kids was massacred by Apaches. Then he just kinda . . ."

"Tennessee boy," another cut in. "I heard the name Travis, somewhere."

"Uh-uh," Jack said. "That ain't it at all. Hell, didn't you yahoos hear the way the man talked? He's got hisself some eddication. I heard his daddy was a big shot back East. Pittsburgh, I think. Made him a pile o' money in steel. But this Desperado character, he didn't want nothin' to do with business. He'd been readin' too many dime novels. Got himself the Ned Buntline bug, chucked ever'thin', an' come out West."

By now everyone was talking, a couple of men arguing over whether or not it was true that the subject of their conversation had ridden with the Clantons, out in Arizona, whether or not he'd butted heads with the Earps. The old man, McGee, claimed that he'd talked to a man who'd told him this Desperado feller had wiped out a whole band of Comanches near San Angelo. Another snorted, said he was obviously too young. "The Comanches've been tamed since seventy-five."

"So what?" someone snapped. "I heard tell he was hell on wheels when he was a kid."

Meanwhile, the stranger, the one they were calling the Desperado, was no more than a few yards away. When he'd left the saloon, he'd mounted his horse and was about to ride out of town. But he did not like the way the saddle was riding, so he guided the animal around to the side of the saloon, where light, spilling from an open window in the saloon's side wall, would give him enough visibility to see what he was doing.

He dismounted, and while he was tightening the saddle girth, he heard most of what was being said inside. He smiled wryly.

People liked telling stories, particularly over things they didn't know much about. And they knew damned little about him. Had no idea of how it had been. What his story really was.

He shook his head, thinking back, remembering a boy's confusion, a boy's pain, as his world collapsed around him.

CHAPTER THREE

She looked so small. And suddenly so old. Her hair had diminished to wisps, plastered against her sweat-slick skull. Her eyes had lost their shine, lay sunken within their orbits. The fever consumed her, hour by hour.

Luther stood near the foot of the bed, a tall, gangly boy, watching as his mother died. His father, Horace, sat on a kitchen chair near his wife's head. Earlier, he had been talking to her, a steady stream of words, increasingly without meaning, but when it became clear she could no longer make sense of any words at all, Horace had fallen silent.

It had been one of those sudden fevers, the kind that strike without warning. And kill quickly. Three days before, Luther's mother had been her usual self, full of life, strong and cheerful. And now she was nearly gone. The suddenness of it had unnerved the boy. That death could strike like that. No wonder death was shown as a reaper, a grim figure with an enormous scythe, mowing down lives like ripening grain.

A moment of rebellion rose inside the boy. Rebellion against man's mortality. It was so wrong! His mother wasn't old yet! Not like old Mrs. Jackson, who'd died last year. His mother should have a long time left. . . .

But life was already leaving her body. Luther watched her final struggle, saw her eyes, their blue color, the same blue as his own eyes, but faded now, come alive for one last time. She turned to her husband, clutched his wrist desperately. "Horace," she whispered, her voice ugly, once a lovely voice, now dried out by the fever. "Horace," she repeated, her voice steadying a little. "Promise me . . . promise you'll make things good for Luther. That you won't . . ."

One last straining away from the bed, her grasp so strong that it left welts on Horace's wrist, then she fell back on the bed. She shuddered once, then Luther heard a sound he'd never forget. His mother's death rattle. One last desperate breath.

Luther could tell, from the sudden slump of his father's shoulders, the half-stifled moan, that it was over. That his mother was dead. Part of him wanted to cry out against it, deny it, but he knew it was true.

Horace got to his feet. Father and son stood by the bed for several minutes, looking down at the body of the woman they had both loved. Then Horace bent over to close his wife's eyes. He straightened up, turned toward Luther. Their eyes locked, then drifted away. Neither cried. Neither had been brought up to cry. Neither had any means of expressing his grief. Each of them had no choice but to keep the pain locked up inside. That was their tradition.

The funeral was held the next day. Not that it was much of a funeral. Only Mrs. Oliphant, from the next farm over, came; she and Luther's mother had been close friends. Word had gotten around that Mrs. McCall had died of the fever, and few wanted to risk their own health. The Reverend Schmidt had shown up, Bible in hand, but Horace had run him off. "Damned if I'll let that twisted hypocrite say anything ugly over Lucy's grave," he had snarled, within Luther's hearing.

So the three of them buried her, Horace, Luther, and Mrs. Oliphant. They buried her on the hill from which she used to watch the sunset. Her favorite place. Horace read words over the grave, not from the Bible, for which he had little use. Instead, he recited an old Greek poem that had been chiseled, two thousand years before, on the grave of a young woman from Athens. Luther did not understand the words, because his father spoke them in Greek, but he liked their sound.

He and his father filled in the grave. And with each shovelful Luther felt as if he were pouring mud onto his own soul.

Afterwards, as day followed day, there was nothing for Luther to do except watch the inevitable come nearer. His father hated the farm, hated farming itself, had often said that only pigs should root in the dirt. Luther knew that the only thing keeping Horace tied to the land was his wife's last words. To care for her son, for Luther. To her, that meant providing security and continuity.

Which translated into the farm. Land. Possessions.

Luther watched his father struggle with the land, and with himself. Watched, as weeks became months, a little bit of life go out of him every day. Before, Luther's mother had been reason enough to stay on the farm. But with her gone . . .

One day Luther and his father were hunched over in the hot sun, hoeing weeds from a field of beets. It was springtime, the air was sweet, green things were shooting up everywhere. Overhead, a flight of geese lay strung out in a vee across the sky, heading north. Both Luther and Horace were filthy and tired. Both straightened up at the same moment. "Paw," Luther said. "I hate farmin', too."

A moment's surprised silence, then springtime broke out all across Horace's face. "Then let's get the hell out of here, son."

It took a month to sell the farm. Horace sold it so cheaply that it might have taken less time, but he wanted to make sure he sold it to someone who would take care of Lucy's grave, up there on her hill. It took another two weeks to sell out personal belongings, and buy equipment for the road, including a pair of good horses and a wagon. Finally they were off, in midsummer, with Horace pointing the horses in the only direction it was possible for him to go. "Out West, Luther," he said to his son, as both sat on the wagon seat. "That's where this country's destiny lies. And our destiny with it."

No surprise at all to Luther. For years his father had pored over every account of the West he could get his hands on; he was an avid reader. He read accounts of explorers and frontiersman, while Luther read Ned Buntline's dime novels. Which had been enough to plant deep in the boy, as well as the father, the desire to see the land about which they had read so much.

Of course, as usual, reality cast its own colors over their dreams. The West was scattered with towns made up mostly of shacks, and the men who had headed West brought Eastern greed with them. Horace was not the mountain man type; he was attracted to small towns at the edge of the wilderness. To actually live in all that immensity, with no one else near, did not appeal to him at all. But it did to Luther. He wondered what it would be like to just take whatever a horse could carry and vanish into the West's empty vastness.

They settled in a small town in Nebraska, where Horace put the money from the farm into a hardware store. Business was good; with his knowledge of farming, Horace was able to anticipate the needs of the local farmers. Always an optimist, Horace began to expand, buying more and more goods. To finance this expansion he borrowed money from the local bank. The banker, a Mr. Chase, was all joviality. He and Horace became friends, often ate together. Sometimes Horace spent half the night in the saloon with Mr. Chase, and came home smelling of whiskey. Although, to Luther, he seldom seemed really drunk.

Life took on an even rhythm. Which Luther found boring. He knew that mountains lay further to the west. The Rocky Mountains. The ones through which Jim Bridger, Kit Carson, Jed Smith, and the other mountain men had wandered, just a generation before. He wanted to see those mountains. The trip west, all those weeks of travelling, with new sights every day, had planted deep inside the boy a hunger to travel just for the sake of travelling.

But his father seemed content, and life was not really so bad. His father had given him a small caliber rifle from the store's stock, and Luther often wandered off into the prairie, potting rabbits and sage hens. During good weather he would sometimes stay out all night, lying on his back, drowsy, minutes from sleep, looking up at the vastness of the Western night sky. Sure beat farming.

Of course, there was school, which he resented while the weather was good, but his father was adamant about school. "A man's future lies in learning," his father told him again and again. "Not only in the things he learns, but in the love of learning. A man without education, a man who does not ask questions about this wonderful world we live in, is not quite a complete man."

So Luther went to school . . . although he wanted to remind his father of Abe Lincoln, who had done his studying at home. But when the harsh Nebraska winter struck, he was glad enough to be in the schoolhouse, with its glowing iron stove and the company of the local boys. And girls. There were some really pretty local girls, and Luther's natural instincts were functioning quite well.

The cold was intense. Luther used the weather as a challenge, and on weekends, when he was not needed at the store, he resumed his hunting trips. There was not much to hunt, but he enjoyed pitting himself against the vast, snowy plains. Once, while he was on his way back to town, a blizzard struck with sudden ferocity. Trusting an inner sense of direction, Luther made it back to the house. Barely. When he finally staggered in through the doorway, exhausted, half-frozen, he could see the concern on his father's face. But Horace said nothing, other than a general, "I'm glad to see you." He was aware that not all the factors in the development of a young man's character were to be found in books.

Then business got bad. An economic depression struck the entire nation, as it did every twenty years or so, in the usual free market boom and bust cycle. Struck everyone, except, of course, the small number of extremely rich men who owned most of the nation's wealth. It was a disaster for the McCalls. The local farmers could no longer afford the supplies they needed. Worse, Horace had extended generous credit, and now the farmers could not pay what they owed.

Horace's debts became due at the bank. He was not able to pay them off. Suddenly Mr. Chase was no longer friendly. First there were warnings, and legal papers, then one day the sheriff tacked a notice onto the store's front door. Mr. Chase had foreclosed.

Horace tried to be understanding. "Business is business," he told Luther.

"But Paw . . . he was your *friend*!"

What was hardest for Horace to accept was the loss of his personal savings. For almost two years he had given Mr. Chase sums of cash, to be put into an account for Luther's future education. Just handed the money over to his friend. And now, when he asked for the money back, Mr. Chase stonily refused to admit that any such money had ever existed.

With no documents to back up his claim, Horace, shaking his head wearily, turned his back on Mr. Chase and walked away. Luther, all youthful rage, wanted to take his rifle and go shoot Mr. Chase. Horace took the rifle away. Luther did go stand in front of the bank for over an hour, staring in through the window, until finally Mr. Chase came outside. Standing beside the front door, he called out, "What the hell do you want, boy?"

Luther stared straight into Mr. Chase's eyes. Strange . . . he'd never before realized how shifty Mr. Chase's eyes were. "To tell you to your face that you're a thief."

Mr. Chase flushed. "Get the hell outta here boy. Before I call the sheriff."

Luther continued staring at Mr. Chase for several more seconds. It was the first time he discovered that there was something in his gaze that disturbed other people. Mr. Chase looked away nervously. Luther turned on his heel and walked away, his heart filled with a loathing for bankers that would last the rest of his life.

Horace and Luther pulled out in the night, in the horse and wagon, taking with them what little goods they had left, before they too were taken from them. "I suppose I was stupid, son," Horace said softly as they crossed the town line, "for having placed such blind trust in a man."

Horace was silent for a moment, then added, "But in a way, there's probably less pain in trusting your fellow man than in living a life that's closed in by fear and suspicion."

Which was when Luther realized fully that his father was a thoroughly impractical man. A dreamer. A man who tried to live by ideals so high, so theoretical, that they went right over the heads of his fellow men. And he got burned. Again and again he would get burned. You gotta think, the boy told himself. Sure, have ideals, but figure out what the other man's ideals are. If he has any.

Luther got to see his mountains. It was early spring. They headed south and west, across more plains. Then, one day, off to the right, Luther saw them. The Rocky Mountains. At first he thought he was looking at a low cloud formation, but as they angled nearer, and the air cleared, he stared in awe at distant, snow-covered peaks. "We gonna head over that way, Paw?" he asked hopefully.

Horace smiled. "Sure son. Straight for Denver."

They turned west. The mountains grew closer and closer, until they half blotted out the western sky. As usual, Horace had his head in a book—a guide to Colorado. "It says here that what we're looking at, those mountains, that's the Front range. Lies behind Denver. Some of the peaks go up to over fourteen thousand feet."

Luther was not particularly impressed by Denver; it was just a big town on its way to becoming a city. The streets were muddy with spring runoff. Traffic was heavy: buggies and stages and big freight wagons on their way to and from the mines that lay further west and south, high up in the mountains.

Luther caught sight of a party of three horsemen. They were wearing buckskins. They had long hair and thick beards, and all carried heavy plains rifles, with single-shot pistols stuck into their leather waistbands. Mountain men. Real mountain men. Never mind that their buckskins were filthy with grease and years of wear, or that their matted hair was probably full of lice, and that they looked meaner than snakes. Real mountain men. Not a one of them under fifty. Old-timers.

The McCalls, father and son, didn't last long in Denver. Thinking of starting some small business with the few goods he had left in the wagon, Horace soon discovered that rents were high in Denver, and competition stiff. Then he began hearing about the mines, up in the mountains, where instant towns were springing up around fabulous ore deposits. Where a barrel of whiskey might bring as much as fifteen hundred dollars profit. All kinds of goods were needed, and few were to be found.

So they left Denver and headed up into the mountains. The trip was an enchantment for Luther. As far as the eye could see—which, admittedly, was not far, since everything seemed to be straight up and down—there was nothing but wilderness. Forests clinging to mountainsides. Deep canyons, with a gleam of water way down at the bottom—the stream that had cut that canyon. He saw startled deer, crashing away through the willows. And once, a bear. An actual grizzly, about 150 yards away, rearing up on its hind legs to take a look at them. Luther noticed how his father's hand involuntarily strayed toward the rifle that now always lay on the seat next to him.

Luther knew the bear wasn't going to charge. He didn't know how he knew, he just felt it inside. So he let his fantasies drift. That rifle so close to his father's hand had to be there because of bandits. In all the dime novels he'd read about the West, there were always bandits. A man had to be ready to defend himself at all times. And now he was *here*, in that very West. The boy felt a deep thrill run through him.

But it was not bandits who eventually robbed them. One afternoon they reached a small town high up in the mountains. A collection of shacks, really, but it had a saloon, and Horace had not tasted whiskey for some time. Nor had he been in adult male company.

So he went into the saloon. Luther waited with the wagon, and while he waited, he looked around. And what he saw he did not like. All the people in sight were men, and they were rough-looking men. He noticed the way some of them were studying the wagon. One man, dirty, with a hideous scar where he'd lost one eye, walked very close and looked inside, pausing for a moment while he tried to make out the goods stacked in the back. Luther's hand strayed toward the rifle. The man, after glaring at him, quickly walked away.

Luther, uncomfortable, picked up the rifle and headed toward the saloon. He stopped at the swinging doors, not wanting to intrude on his father. But something warned him, something about this town. . . .

Peering in over the doors—he was now almost six feet tall, although thin as a rail—Luther saw his father. He was standing at the bar, a glass in his hand. Luther could tell by the way his father stood, the tension in his body, that things were not going well. Several men stood around him, and they did not look friendly. Then Luther saw the man with the missing eye come in the back door. He whispered something to a couple of other men, then they all closed in around Horace.

Which was not that easy. Dreamer that he was, Horace was a powerful man, and not at all cowardly. He rang a coin down onto the bar top. "Settling up," he said, and started to turn toward the door.

But two of the men stepped into his path. "Well, Mr. Fancy Talker, where the hell do you think you're goin'?" one asked, his voice a half-snicker.

"Outside," Horace said quietly, starting to step between the two men in front of him, unaware that the one-eyed pug-ugly and another man had closed in behind him. One of the men in front put out a hand to stop him. Horace pushed it away, jerked the man past him, started to pass by, when one of men behind punched him in the back of the head.

Horace staggered forward, almost went down, but caught himself. One of the men started to kick him. Horace moved to the side, evaded the kick, and hit the man in the face with his fist, so hard that the man went flying backward until he hit a table and went down with chairs scattering all around him.

Perhaps Horace could have made it to the door, but Luther, by the doorway, saw the one-eyed man, behind Horace, produce a long, thin-bladed knife. The kind they called an Arkansas toothpick.

Luther acted without wasting time thinking. He had a rifle in his hand, a Winchester Yellow Boy repeater, in .44 caliber rimfire. He cranked back the hammer, pulled the butt against his shoulder, and fired over the door, right at the one-eyed man.

In his haste, he missed, but the roar of the shot reverberated all around the room. Everyone froze in place, including Horace, who looked first at Luther, staring, then turned to look behind him and saw the man with the knife. Then Horace was moving, straight for the doors. "Thanks, son," he said, taking the rifle from Luther. He worked the loading lever; Luther, having shot at a man for the first time in his life, had forgotten to jack another shell into the chamber.

There were yells from inside the saloon, but no one seemed anxious to show himself in the doorway. Horace and Luther walked quickly toward their wagon. They were just about to climb aboard, indeed, Luther already had one foot on the step, when a voice called out, "What the hell's goin' on? Who fired that shot?"

Luther and Horace turned. Two men were approaching with rapid strides. Both wore old cavalry pistols in worn holsters, and both had badges pinned to their vests. "You there," the same man snapped. "What are you doing with that rifle?"

"Some trouble in the saloon," Horace replied. "Some men tried to, well . . . I think . . . rob me."

"That's a lie, Sheriff," a voice sang out from the saloon's doorway. The one-eyed man was standing just outside the swinging doors. "Fella started trouble. Then the young 'un, he opened up on us."

The sheriff's eyes locked onto Horace. "That so?"

"Not at all, Sheriff. They . . . ."

The sheriff, close now, held out his hand. "Better give me that rifle."

Luther, this close, got a good look at the sheriff. He didn't like what he saw; he had the same mean look about him as the men in the saloon. Indeed, the whole town had that look. "Don't do it, Paw," he said. "Let's just drive on out."

Horace hesitated for a moment. The sheriff had his right hand close to his gun butt. So did the other man with him. Luther figured that must be his deputy, just like in the books. Horace sighed, relaxed. "They're the law, son. It's wrong to buck the law."

He handed over the rifle. The sheriff smiled, then, reversing the rifle, sank the butt into Horace's stomach. "Next time, mister," he said, grinning, "be a little quicker about doin' what I say."

Luther started forward, but his father, gasping for breath, nevertheless had enough strength to hold out an arm, blocking his way. "No, son. We wouldn't gain anything at all."

They were marched away to a makeshift jail, a log hut with one window so small that no one over the age of five would be able to get through it. The door slammed behind them, cutting of most of the light. There was one bunk. Luther could smell it from all the way across the room. He watched as his father walked over to the small window and looked out. The window was high on the wall, so Horace had to stand on tiptoe. One long look, then Horace turned to face his son. "Guess the West isn't working out too well for us."

"Ah, Paw. . . ."

"No, listen. Thanks again for firing that shot. It may have saved my life."

"Maybe if I'd just sung out. . . ."

Horace shook his head. "No. I don't think that would have done it. Don't blame yourself. The fault was mine. For going into that saloon. In a town I didn't know."

Even in the dim light, Luther could make out his father's wry smile. "There's more than one way that old Demon Rum can take a man down."

They spent the night in the jail, huddled together in a corner, neither caring to lay down on the reeking bed. In the morning they were marched, between the sheriff and his deputy, to a rickety building. A sign out front read, "Lemuel Johnson," and under that, "Justice of the Peace."

Lemuel Johnson was a seedy little man, sitting behind a plank desk. A bottle of whiskey was one of the few items on top of the desk. Lemuel Johnson looked up as the McCalls and the sheriff and his deputy came in. "Well . . . what we got today, Zeke?" he asked the sheriff.

"Assault with a deadly weapon. Shootin' up the saloon. Near put a hole in Snake-Eye."

The justice of the peace nearly smiled. "Too bad they missed."

The sheriff actually did smile. "Someone won't, someday."

Which put hope into the McCalls. Maybe they'd get a medal, and be sent on their way. But their hope was short-lived. Lemuel Johnson reached for the bottle, took a swig, then got down to business. "How do you plead?" he asked Horace.

"Not guilty."

Lemuel took another sip of his whiskey. "Well, that there's just downright too bad. Cause I find you guilty as charged."

"But," Horace burst out, "we didn't have a chance to tell our side. . . ."

The sheriff punched Horace in the kidneys. "Shut your mouth, stranger. Nobody asked your opinion."

Now Luther stepped forward. "But it was me!" he burst out. "I fired the shot. They were gonna stab my father in the back!"

The sheriff took a step toward Luther. Horace turned, and there was something about the look on his face that made the sheriff back off.

"Well, hell, I'll find you both guilty, then," the justice of the peace said, fingering his bottle. He turned toward the sheriff. "Whatta they got, Zeke?"

"Not much. A wagon. Some horses. Junk inside the wagon. The rifle."

The justice of the peace sighed, then, picking up the whiskey bottle, he slammed the bottom of it down on the desk as if it were a gavel. "Well, that's it, then. My sentence is that these two yahoos be fined one wagon, the horses that go with that wagon, and everything inside that wagon."

The sheriff raised his arms up as if he were firing a rifle. "Oh," Lemuel Johnson amended, "and one rifle."

Then, silence. Luther wanted to cry out against the injustice of it all. But his father, who, just like Luther, had now lost everything, was standing with quiet dignity. Luther felt he must do the same.

"You're free to go now," Johnson said. He started to reach for his bottle, then pulled his hand away. "But if I was you, I'd think real hard about gettin' outta town. Real fast."

The sheriff was shepherding them out now. Luther turned, looked straight at the man. Once again, as with Mr. Chase, something in Luther's gaze caused the other man to turn away. And, as with Mr. Chase and bankers, Luther felt, growing inside of him, a loathing for all sheriffs. One he knew he'd never get over.

CHAPTER FOUR

Walking. One foot in front of the other, until boots began to wear out. Walking further up into the mountains, always heading west.

The sheriff, perhaps in a good mood after having made such a coup, had permitted Horace and Luther to take some of their clothing from the wagon. Horace had made packs out of old blankets, and now they trudged along, like two tramps, growing a little more ragged each day, a little more gaunt. And in a land that was suffering an invasion of the ambitious, anyone down on his luck could expect short shrift. They were chased away from homesteads, taken for thieves. Horace remarked to his son one day that he supposed they certainly looked fearsome enough.

After the arrest, Horace still had a little money tucked away in a hidden pocket of his trousers. But very little. For two weeks it sufficed to buy them enough to eat. After that, hunger began to bite at their bellies.

That was the hardest part for Luther; he did not like being hungry. After the humiliation of being arrested and robbed had worn off, the boy had discovered that he did not particularly mind their new situation. Riding in a wagon through the mountains had been one thing, walking on foot quite another. He was that much closer to the ground, more aware of everything around him. He did miss the rifle. Game abounded; they could have eaten well if they'd been armed. And if they'd been armed, Luther swore to himself, that sheriff would have something to worry about. He'd go back, make it come out even. His father respected the law. Luther did not. Not anymore.

One day they saw a cabin uphill from the trail. Horace eyed it speculatively. His stomach ached with hunger. He hated the thought of asking anyone for a handout, would probably never have done it for himself alone, but he saw how pale Luther was. He felt a twinge of guilt. He'd promised the boy's mother he'd take good care of him. And now the boy was starving. "Come on," he said. "Let's give it a try."

The cabin was a poor-looking place, rudely constructed, made of rough planking, old enough so that the wind had pushed it over to the leeward side. The McCalls trudged wearily up the steep slope below the cabin. They were about thirty yards away when the front door opened a crack. "Who the hell are ye?" someone demanded in a cracked voice. "Sing out, or ol' Betsy here, she's agonna cut loose."

Horace stopped, reached out to stop Luther. He could just make out the shadowy form of someone behind that partially open door, and, at about latch level, the muzzle of a gun. "Just two wanderers," Horace called out. "Hungry and tired."

For the first time since they'd left the farm Horace's shoulders slumped. It looked like they were going to be turned away again. Then the cabin door opened wider, and a man stepped out into the open, an old man, as his voice had indicated, grizzled, but not stooped. He was wearing rough buckskin clothing, and, of all things, an actual coonskin cap. The old rifle he was holding looked to be about the same vintage as the coonskin. "You armed?" the old man asked suspiciously.

"Not anymore," Luther replied.

"Why, I'll be damned," the old man said, progressively less hostile, "you ain't more'n a boy."

"A hungry boy," Horace put in.

"Well, hell," the old man said, resting his rifle butt on the ground. "Figure we kin do somethin' about that."

His name was Seth. He had food, and within half an hour Horace and Luther were digging into a hearty venison stew, while old Seth talked their ears off. Living alone, he was eager for conversation.

He told them, "Come up here years ago when there warn't nothin' but critturs. An' a few redskins, ready to lift a man's hair. I come after the beaver. But, the beaver's all gone. The redskins, too. Never thought I'd miss them Injuns, but I surely do. They knew this land, knew how to use it. Now we got them damn market hunters, killin' off the last o' the critturs. An' a passel o' greenhorns, up here to make their pile. No offense meant, fellers."

When Seth heard the story of their run-in with the sheriff, he snorted angrily. "Heard about that yahoo. Someday somebody's gonna put a hole in him."

They stayed a week at the cabin. Seth took a particular shine to Luther. "Reminds me o' myself, back when," he told Horace. "When I first come out here. He's got the feel of the land all the way through him."

By the end of the week it was time to move on. The West was still out there, and Seth, despite the opportunity to beat his gums, was feeling a little pressured by all this human company. "It'll start gettin' cold in another few weeks," he told Horace on the last day. "You're gonna have to find a place to hole up."

"I suppose I'll have to get a job," Horace admitted.

"Ain't much work up in these mountains. 'Ceptin' minin'."

"I guess I could do that."

"Awful work," Seth said, looking away. "Course, workin' for other people in general is about as . . . well, like I said, there ain't much except minin' up here. Know of a mine about two days hike up the trail. They're always needin' people. Run through 'em like . . . well, never mind."

So they pushed on. Two days later they were approaching the mine Seth had told them about. They could tell something big lay ahead by the increased wagon traffic along the trail. And by the growing cloud of dust in the near distance. A muted pounding began to invade their heads, like the pounding of the blood in a man's veins. Topping a rise, they saw the mine itself, spread out below them, a quarter of a mile away.

They both stopped in their tracks. It was a full minute before either could say anything. "My God," Horace finally murmured.

After weeks of rambling through nearly untouched wilderness, the devastation below was appalling. The mine lay in a valley about a mile long and a third of a mile across. From the stumps, they could see that the entire area had once been heavily wooded, but every tree in sight had been cut down. The resulting erosion had gullied the slopes above the valley floor. Even from a quarter of a mile away they could see the thick mud that lay in every low spot. Huge mounds of mine tailings disfigured the valley floor. A pall of dirty smoke hung over the entire area, pouring from chimneys and smokestacks. Large, ugly buildings, constructed of weathered planking, lay at the center of the valley, and around those larger buildings, a sprawl of shacks and outhouses.

Luther looked down, looked up again. "Paw," he asked, "how could anybody do . . ."

"Progress, son," Horace replied. "The glorious nineteenth century. Mankind's finest hour. Or so they tell us . . . the people who make places like this."

They started down the slope. The meager provisions old Seth had given them had run out that morning. Horace knew he'd have to find some kind of work, or they'd starve. He began to point out features. "See that really tall building? Probably the pithead. There's lifting machinery in there, cables running down into the shaft."

Now that they were closer, the pounding sound was louder. "Stamp mill," Horace guessed. "Crushing the ore."

They reached the valley floor. The mud was a thick stinking glue. They tried to avoid it, but their boots were sucked down into clinging muck. The stench of the entire place, the mud, the polluted air, seared their lungs, which were quite unprepared for all this magnificent progress after the clean air of the wilderness.

Now men were around them. Tired-looking men, very dirty men. A few looked at them curiously, but most just looked down at the ground, moving by in an exhausted trance. They found the mine office easily enough; it was the best building in sight. The hiring process was simple. A gimlet-eyed clerk snapped that, yes, they did need men. Had Horace ever done any mining? When he answered no, he was hired anyhow. "Since you aren't experienced, you start at two dollars a day. If you pan out, you go up to three."

The clerk turned toward Luther. "And as for the boy . . ."

"He's not going down the mine," Horace snapped. "He's still school age."

The clerk smiled. Smirked, rather. "No schools around here. And every swingin' dick earns his keep."

He looked Luther up and down. "Big kid. There's some of 'em younger than him that—"

"He's not going down the mine," Horace repeated firmly.

The clerk shrugged. "Okay. They need a swamper over at the mess hall." He looked up at Horace, his face cold. "I hope you ain't gonna tell me he's too good for that, too."

"No, that's fine," Horace said. He was suddenly very tired. He was a long way from the farm, a longer way from his dreams. Perhaps in a few months, after they'd holed up here for the winter, they'd have some money saved up, enough to push on. Maybe they'd go on out to California. Maybe. Anywhere but here.

They were shown to a sagging shack; the mining company provided housing for its employees. As Horace and Luther were to find out, this particular valley was unlike the normal Colorado mining operation. Generally, there were many mines in a given area, different strikes, claimed by various individuals. Towns grew up around those strikes, wide-open towns, full of wild individualism.

Not this mine. The entire valley, and the land for miles around, had been purchased by a single individual, a wealthy Scot. There was one mine, one town. All belonging to one man. Duncan Fife. And Duncan Fife ran his little Western empire like a medieval Scottish fiefdom. The men lived in company shacks, ate company food, and, when their own clothing ran out, had no choice but to buy from the company store. All on credit. Which came out of their wages. And since prices were high in the company store, and wages low, there was seldom much left over. Many of the men were in debt to the mine.

Which was more or less bearable to Horace. After all, they would get through the winter with food in their bellies and some protection against the weather. In the springtime he'd manage somehow to accumulate enough money to push on. He even thought of buying a rifle from the company store . . . until he discovered that rifles were not available. The Scot, in the European tradition, was not about to let the working class arm itself.

The ordeal began. It was not so bad for Luther; he spent several hours a day swamping out the mess hall. In return, he received his meals. Horace's meals were taken out of his pay—if, at the end of his shift, he had the strength left to eat. The mine was worked in two twelve-hour shifts. Horace was assigned to the night shift, going down the mine at eight, and coming back up at eight in the morning. Usually, he fell straight into bed. Sometimes, in the evening, before he went back down the hole, he'd tell Luther about it. "It's a deep mine," he said one day, as he dressed. "I've been working at over two thousand feet. The heat is terrible. We work half an hour on, half an hour off. Not because Fife is a kind man, but because the men would collapse otherwise. He makes sure he gets every penny's worth out of us."

The heat. Horace was always talking about the heat. "It's a steam bath down there. Some of the rocks are too hot to touch. I saw a man get scalded the other day. His drill went through into a pocket of water. Boiling water. The drill came shooting out of the hole because of the pressure. It could have taken his head off. As soon as the drill was out of the hole, there was a big gusher of hot water. Peeled away half his hide."

Little by little, Luther began to get a picture of the mine. His father told him it was a carbonate mine. Carbonate of lead, containing silver. "Mucky stuff," Horace said, grimacing. "You can't shore it up the regular way. It would just crumble down around the shoring. So some German engineer designed these huge open boxes, made out of timbers. They just stack them on top of one another, all the way up to the ceiling. Makes the place look like the inside of a beehive. They call them Deidesheimer Squares, after the man who invented them."

Luther's mind was busy building an image of a murky underground hell. Which, of course, he was eager to see for himself. One day he got his chance. Duncan Fife himself was in the mess hall. He sometimes ate there to save a few pennies; he was a miserly man. But he was not eating at the moment. He needed to send a message down the mine to one of his foremen. He caught sight of Luther. "What's that man doin' above ground and out of bed during the day shift?" he asked peevishly.

"Swamper," the cook answered.

Fife walked up to Luther. He was a medium-sized man, thin rather than slender. His expression fascinated Luther. Cold without being tough. The coldness of greed and lack of concern for his fellow man. Lack of concern for anything other than personal profit. Beady little eyes.

Fife subjected Luther to a short, silent, intense inspection. As if I were some kind of mine machinery he was thinking of buying, Luther thought. Fife finally spoke. "You're younger than I thought when I first saw the brawn o' ye. But ye'll do ta carry a message for me, boy."

So for the first time Luther entered the huge lift house. It was several stories high, towering over the pithead, a single vast room, filled to the roof with the lifting machinery. A huge steam engine pounded away, turning enormous spools of wire. For several minutes Luther just stood, gaping, watching the engine's huge flywheel, which was easily twenty feet across, slowly turning. The massive steam cylinders filled the shed with a heavy chuffing sound.

"Hey, boy!" someone shouted. "Get your finger outta yer ass, or the damned cage is gonna go down without you."

Luther turned away from the engines, then walked toward the pithead. The pit itself, the mine's main vertical shaft, was a ragged black hole in the ground, with tendrils of steam rising slowly out of the darkness below. A metal cage hung suspended above the pit by heavy wire cables. Several men were already inside, ready for the trip down into the mine. The man who'd yelled took Luther's arm, hustled him into the cage. The cage swayed. Luther snatched at the metal bars. The man laughed. "Seasick, kid?"

Someone called out. Luther turned, saw that it was the lift cage operator, sitting surrounded by levers and dials. The man next to Luther shouted back, "Ready to go down!"

Luther saw the lift operator nod, then slam a lever forward. With horrible suddenness the cage floor fell away from below Luther. He choked back a cry of terror. They were falling, the cage and everyone in it, falling with a frightening velocity. There was blackness outside the cage, broken by an occasional shaft of dim light each time they passed the entrance to a lighted horizontal tunnel. Then, back into blackness.

Luther started to wrap an arm through and around the steel bars. A man pulled him back. "Anything you stick outside this cage, sonny, you're gonna lose."

"Yeah," another man said with a snicker. "Don't try peein' between the bars, or you ain't never gonna have no kids."

Suddenly the cage jerked to a halt. For a few seconds it bounced up and down on the wire from which it was suspended. They were at the entrance to one of the horizontal tunnels. Luther remembered that the miners called them drifts. Two men got off. The cage door was shut, a line tugged, then they were falling again. "How does the man running the machine know where to stop?" Luther asked one of the miners.

"Got hisself a big dial attached to the drum," the miner drawled laconically. "Tells him the depth."

Down and down they went. Luther began to tug at the collar of his shirt. The heat was becoming intense. A wet, clinging heat. Suffocating. The air felt thick; it was hard to breathe. My God, he wondered, how did a man actually do any work down in this hell?

Luther was let off at one of the lowest drifts. At the pithead he'd been given a miner's hat with a lamp attached, which helped him while he was passing through the narrower, darker part of the drift, then he stepped into an enormous room which was lit by dozens of lamps attached to the walls. And now he saw the Deidesheimer

Squares, in sets, huge open boxes made of heavy timbers, just like his father had said, stacked all the way up to the ceiling. Which Luther could barely make out. The ceiling, the walls, seemed to soak up the light. He had been expecting glittering ore, instead, he saw a blue-black material that was obviously quite crumbly. He shuddered, imagining all that muck bursting through the squares, falling, crushing him under its immense, smothering weight.

He was delivering his message to the foreman when he saw his father. Horace was swinging a sledgehammer, slamming it against the butt of a long metal drill, which a second man was holding against the face of the drift. They had obviously encountered hard rock; sparks were flying from the point of the drill.

Luther studied his father. He was nearly naked, wearing nothing but a pair of shorts. His body was caked with grime. Runnels of sweat had cut paths through the grime. Luther was aware, for the first time, how thin his father had become, how tired he looked.

A whistle blew. Horace dropped the hammer, walked over to a water bucket, poured a dipper of water over his head, then drank a second dipperful. A boy came running with something. Luther saw that it glittered. Silver ore? No. Ice. Luther watched his father put the ice in his mouth and suck gratefully.

Uncomfortable, feeling as if he'd been spying on his father's deepest secrets, Luther started to step behind some timbering. But his father saw the movement, turned, stared for a moment, then his face clouded. He came walking over to Luther. "What are you doing down here?" he demanded.

"He sent me with a message," Luther blurted. He had never seen such anger on his father's face.

"Sent you? Who sent you?"

"Mr. Fife. He was in the mess hall. There wasn't anyone else. . . ."

Horace's expression lost some of its anger. "Ah, well. I suppose you had to see this hell for yourself someday."

His expression hardened again. "Now . . . get back up on top. And if that son of a bitch ever tries to send you down here again, you tell him to come and talk to me first."

Luther nodded, then turned and went straight back to the lift cage. "It'll be a wait, bub," a miner told him. "Went up maybe ten minutes ago. Should be at the pithead about now."

He was an old miner, maybe fifty, which Luther had learned was a lot of years for a man to carry to this kind of work. Most of the man's teeth were missing. His skin was weathered, yet it had probably seldom felt actual weather.

They were all standing, waiting for the cage, about a dozen men altogether, when, from far up the shaft, Luther became aware of a faint sound, a distant wail, a long, ululating cry, coming nearer. Coming with great speed.

The old miner had heard it, too. Luther watched the man's face blanch. "Oh, God, not again," the miner half-whispered.

"What . . . ?" Luther started to say.

"Some poor devil's fallen down the shaft."

One more scream, nearer now, suddenly cutting off with a grunt as the man's body began hitting obstructions. Horrible, wet, smashing sounds. Then, a grisly rain. Bits and pieces of man came into sight, falling past Luther, landing in the steaming water of the sump at the foot of the shaft. One piece spun into the drift, landing not five feet from Luther. An arm. He was staring at part of a human arm.

The men around Luther were looking everywhere but at the arm. No one seemed to be doing anything about it. Finally, the cage came. They all filed inside. "How . . . ?" Luther started to ask the old miner.

"It's the change in altitude. In the air," the man said gruffly. "Thick down here. Heavy. Hot. Sometimes, when a man gets to the top, all that thin, cool, clean air makes him dizzy. And he falls. Hits things on the way down."

The old miner spat through the cage's bars. "No safety rails up above," he said. For just a minute bitterness crept into his voice. "Safety rails cost money, an' . . . well, never mind."

He was silent for a moment. "They usually fall into the sump at the bottom of the shaft. What's left of 'em. Real hot water in that sump. Cooks a man real slow. They hafta fish out the chunks with hooks."

The old man shook his head violently. When he finally turned back to face Luther, they were at the pithead. Luther could now make out the man's features clearly. He had a sardonic, self-mocking smile on his face. "That's how it all ends for a miner, sonny. Stew. Miner stew."

He leaned close to Luther. "I hear it's a Scotch delicacy. Miner stew. Makes old man Fife's mouth water. Smells like money to the sorry bastard."

CHAPTER FIVE

"Were you still in the mine when Paul Johnson fell down the shaft?"

Luther had known his father was going to ask. Had known it ever since his father had opened the bottle of whiskey and started drinking, sitting slumped over in one of the shack's two rickety chairs, elbows on the splintery pine table. Luther realized he had never seen his father actually sit down and work at a bottle of whiskey before.

"Yeah, Paw. I was there. I . . . heard him fall."

He did not want to say what he had actually seen. About the arm. The rain of blood and flesh.

"Fife doesn't care at all," Horace said half under his breath. "Doesn't give a damn about the safety of the men who make him rich."

He looked up at his son. "Did you know they're cutting back on the shoring in the drifts? Fife claims it costs too much to haul in timber . . . now that they've cut down all the trees around here. He . . . oh, hell, Fife is no different than the rest of those money-grubbing bastards. And with the Republicans in office . . ."

Luther nodded obediently. Republicans were his father's bête noire. Horace had originally voted for Lincoln, for the Republicans, and now felt betrayed. "I should have known better," he muttered, pouring himself another glass of whiskey. "They said it straight out, that they were for industry. And up to a point, they were right. The United States needs industry. But my God, not at the expense of everything else! They've turned the whole country over to people like Duncan Fife to plunder for their own profit."

Horace laughed wryly. "Thomas Jefferson is probably spinning in his grave. He had a dream, a vision of a nation of proud, free farmers, owning their own land. A dead dream now. Hell," he snorted. "We're becoming a nation of wage slaves. The Republicans freed the Negro, now they're selling the workingman to the plutocrats."

"You think the President is a crook, Paw?" Anything to keep his father's mind off the mine.

Horace scratched his chin. Unshaven bristle rasped loudly. He shook his head. "No, I don't think so, son. Not consciously. He's just out of his element. Grant was a fine general, but he's putty in the hands of those party hacks. I think most of the corruption goes on behind Grant's back. But still, that's no excuse. He's the President. He should make it his business to know."

He took a big drink of the whiskey. "Mark my word. As long as Republicans are in power, the workingman will suffer. They . . ."

He had started to take another drink, but stopped with the glass halfway to his mouth. He held it away from him, looked at the amber liquid. "What the hell am I doing?" he murmured. "Damn . . . I'm letting them buy me off with drunken dreams."

He turned toward his son. "You know, don't you, that Fife keeps the price of whiskey and tobacco low in the company store? I guess he figures that if he keeps us drunk enough, keeps our minds dulled, we won't have the courage to speak out."

He got up, poured the whiskey into the wash pan, stuck the cork back into the bottle. "No," he said, more to himself than to Luther. "A man who wants to keep his self respect doesn't blot out his mind. He fights back."

He turned around, looking straight at Luther, and Luther knew he was talking to him directly now. "I'm going to fight back, Luther. I'm going to start acting like a man again."

"Ah, Paw. . . ."

A few of the men had begun whispering about forming a union. Unions had been gaining momentum back East, despite broken heads from company goons. Despite the hiring of Pinkerton strikebreakers. Despite the unbending hostility of the government. Horace began to emerge as the mine's union spokesman. Little by little he spoke out . . . about the mine's horrible accident record. About general working conditions. Much to his surprise, few listened at first. Most of the miners seemed to accept danger as part of their job. No matter how many times Horace told them that it could be much better, only a few listened.

Duncan Fife was not unaware of the few union activists. His foremen began to come to him with disturbing news. But Fife refused to panic. "They know who fills their bellies," he said confidently. He had reason to feel confident. A terrible economic depression had swept the nation. A man with any job at all had to count himself lucky, no matter how miserable the job. One of the really big economic collapses that would sweep the country for the next sixty years had the workingman by the throat. Every twenty years, more or less, boom, then bust.

Then Fife made a mistake. Overestimating the docility of his workers, perhaps remembering the slavish obedience of the British working class, he decided to cut wages by a dollar a day. Now Horace and the few other union sympathizers had the mens' attention. Committees began to form. A delegation approached Fife, who refused to meet with them. "No one's goin' ta tell me what ta do with me own property!" he raged. "Get back ta work, or start walkin'!"

The men did go back to work, although grumbling continued. The weather turned cold. Very cold. In part this was a plus for Fife, because few men wanted to be turned out, jobless, into the bitter mountain cold. But on the other hand, disease began to increase. Coming up from the steamy heat of the mine into the icy winter air gave many men pneumonia. Two died. Others were complaining of rheumatism. The nearest doctor was two days away.

There were rumblings about a strike. And now Duncan Fife knew he had to act quickly. News had come of union trouble back East, where there had been more than one instance of workers successfully gaining ground against greedy industrialists. The men felt heartened, Fife, desperate.

The easiest defense would have been to simply fire the men that Fife considered ringleaders. He thought of them as mutineers, rebelling against the God-given principle of private property. But he knew that they might just as easily, in these trying times, be replaced by other men even more bitter. No. He would prefer to break the troublemakers, crush their spirit, and let the other men see them broken.

So he sent for a small squad of hired goons, men who held the title of foremen, but gave no direct orders. Big men, who stalked the mine and the narrow alleys between the shacks, intimidating the miners by their size and the ugliness of their expressions.

Some of the activists continued to agitate. One morning two were found badly beaten. One of the beaten men, when he had recovered sufficiently, went meekly back to work. The other left the valley. But the majority of the miners were still angry over the cut in their wages. A wage cut was a much more visible symbol than vague talk about possible safety standards, so those who still had the courage to speak out were listened to. The mood grew uglier.

One of those speaking out was Horace McCall. He seemed, to Luther, to have regained a great deal of his old spark, his cheerfulness. Once again he had a dream to follow.

Then he too was attacked. But Horace was ready. He was a big man, powerful. He had hidden a length of drill bit inside his trousers, and when two goons jumped him on his way out of the mine, he pulled out the drill bit and beat them unconscious.

Word of Horace's stand spread through the mine. Now the men knew that Fife and his goons were not all-powerful. The men began to take heart. They had a symbol, a leader; Horace McCall. A man of stature. Many were ready to follow his lead.

Although Horace said nothing to Luther about his fight with the goons, Luther knew soon enough. In the mess hall, men who knew he was Horace's son clapped him on the back. "Some hombre, that old man o' yers."

Luther was proud of his father's courage. But he was also worried. He remembered his earlier encounter with Duncan Fife. Remembered the unbridled greed in the man's face, the ruthlessness that glittered in his eyes, the sense of total conviction. After all, had not Fife's cold, ruthless Calvinist God promised success to the righteous? To men of property? And was not Duncan Fife a righteous man, holding in deep scorn all those who did not prosper as his God had allowed him, in his righteousness, to prosper?

"Paw . . . maybe you better be kinda careful," Luther said one evening, as they sat in their freezing shack. "That Mr. Fife. . . . You could get, well, hurt."

Horace nodded. "You're right, son. I could even get killed."

"But then, well, is it worth it?"

Horace took a moment to rub his chin. "I think so," he finally said. "I'm aware of what can happen, and I've made myself stop and think, and this is what I've come up with. To lose one's life, or to be injured, is a terrible thing, son. But I believe, as much as I've ever believed anything, that to lose one's courage, one's manhood, to kowtow to a poisonous little toad like Duncan Fife, is far worse. To surrender what you believe in, to become another man's slave, to give up your dignity, is the worst thing I can imagine happening to a man. Worse than death itself."

Horace was looking straight at Luther. He said nothing more, but Luther knew that his father was asking for his opinion. Luther nodded. "Yeah, Paw," he finally said. "I guess you're right."

Luther never forgot his father's words; they became the principle on which he based the rest of his life. Those words were Horace McCall's final legacy to his son. That night Horace "fell" down the mine shaft. Or so said the four company goons who had been the only ones with him at the time.

His body was brought to the surface, more or less intact, although the face was badly damaged. Luther watched as they lay his father inside a cheap pine coffin. The carpenter was about to nail the lid shut. "No," Luther said. "Leave it open."

"But," the carpenter said, "his face. . . ."

Luther shook his head. "I want them all to see him that way. See what they did to him."

"Boy . . ." the carpenter said warningly, but the fierceness of the look Luther gave him caused him to fall silent.

Usually, when a man was killed in the mine, he more or less disappeared from general view. But Horace McCall had a regular funeral, the men insisted on it, and Duncan Fife decided to humor the men. A mistake. The funeral was held in the lift house. For the first time anyone could remember, all the miners were above ground at the same time. Mine operations were shut down. Luther stood near the coffin, heard the usual platitudes from a preacher Fife had brought in for the occasion. Soft words designed to lessen the general tension. But the men had seen Horace's ruined face. The tension remained high.

When the preacher had finished, Fife made a sign that the coffin was to be taken away. His plan was to inform the men that there would be whiskey for all, with the rest of the day off, although the words would taste like gall in his mouth. Lost production!

But Luther anticipated him. He stepped up next to the coffin, stood straight, his face grave. "I want to say a few words before my father is buried," he said.

His voice was strong and clear. It carried all through the lift house. The men, some of whom had been murmuring about the rumor of free booze, fell silent. Luther let the silence build for a moment, just long enough. He saw Fife motioning to some of his goons to step in front of Luther. Luther moved around them. "You all knew my father," he said, surprised at the calmness of his voice. "He was a good man. He cared about what happened to the people working this mine. Every individual one of you. He had the courage to speak out. He stuck up for his fellow workers."

Luther let a moment's silence pass. Duncan Fife was glaring at him. Luther looked back, met his stare. Fife tried to hold his gaze, failed, looked away. Luther turned back toward the men. "Because of my father's courage, because of his concern for you, he died. There's not a man here who believes my father fell down the shaft. Every one of us knows he was killed. Murdered. And we know who murdered him."

Luther turned, pointed straight at Duncan Fife and the company goons who surrounded him. "Those men."

Fife was turning purple with rage. "You had better shut your . . ." he started to say.

Luther was speaking again. Not loudly, but his voice carried, cutting through Fife's angry squeak. He was still looking straight at Fife and his goons. "And you'll pay," he said, his voice whip-crack hard now. "Every one of you, you'll pay for what you did. That's a promise."

Pandemonium broke out. Miners came up and pounded Luther on the back. He caught one last glimpse of Duncan Fife's face, saw the rage distorting it. Then he could no longer see Fife. He let a rush of miners carry him out of the lift house, toward the little cemetery where his father would be buried. "You better watch your back, boy," an old miner muttered. "You said some pretty tough words back there."

"And I meant them," Luther said grimly. He thought back over the last two years. His mother's death. The way the banker had swindled them. The sheriff who had stolen their belongings, humiliated them. And now, the man who had taken his father from him. All for greed. Yes, there was payment due. A great deal of payment.

The burial was brief. And now the mood turned again. Luther didn't know what he had hoped for from the miners. A lynching? Duncan Fife swinging over the pithead? Not likely. The whiskey had been brought out. The men began drinking. There was mut-tering at first against Fife, but the whiskey had been a good ploy; the men began to laugh and joke and cut up. Luther walked away; no one seemed to see him go. The day had started with death, now it was full of drink. The miners, facing death every day, wanted its memory blotted out..So they drank, and, at least for the moment, forgot.

Luther knew that it was time for him to start moving. That old miner had been right; he was in danger. He remembered the look on Duncan Fife's face. A killing look.

He went back to the shack. He began throwing his few belongings into an old blanket. What should he take? He considered his father's books. No, too heavy. But they were all he had left to remember him by.

It was a decision he did not have to make. The door suddenly crashed open behind him. Half a dozen men poured in through the doorway. Company goons. Luther reached for the poker, the only weapon he could think of, but he was too late. A heavy fist crashed into the side of his face, and he reeled back, stunned. The goons crowded in close, fists and boots swinging.

Luther never had much of a chance, but he remembered his father's last words, and did not give up. He fought back hard, and had the satisfaction of knowing he hurt some of the men beating him. He kept swinging until he finally fell, semi-conscious. Even as he lay on the rough floor, boots thudded against his ribs and belly.

Suddenly the beating stopped. Luther managed to open one swollen eye. Duncan Fife was standing just inside the shack's doorway. "Filthy hole," Fife murmured, looking around the shack's single room, as if he himself were not responsible for its poor condition.

Unable to move, slipping in and out of consciousness, Luther watched as Fife moved around the room. Fife began to paw through the pile of Horace's books, the few he'd managed to save from the sheriff. Fife picked one up. Plato's *Symposium*. "Pagan trash," Fife snorted. "Burn them all. Burn the shack, too. Let the rest of those worthless scum take it for a warning."

Fife was standing directly over Luther now. He prodded the boy with his boot. It hurt, but Luther refused to groan. "And as for this garbage, he's bad blood," Fife said, his voice ugly with hate. "Get rid of him."

The boot was no longer there. How long it had been gone, Luther did not know. He kept passing out. He did hear pages being torn out of his father's books, heard the first of the flames licking at the shack, and then he was being hoisted up. He could not keep from crying out. "Tough little bastard," he heard one of the men snicker. "Guess he hurts a bit, though."

"Not for long," another replied.

Luther was vaguely aware of being thrown across the back of a horse, or maybe a mule. It was dark outside; he could not quite open his swollen eyes. More pain as the animal started off, led by someone on a horse. An eternity of agony, jolting along a trail, mercifully unconscious part of the time. Then, no longer moving, a voice saying, "Tip him off." Suddenly he was falling, body tensing, waiting for the shock of hitting the ground. But the landing was soft, cushioned. He moved a little. Felt something cool against his face. It felt good. Then it began to feel uncomfortably cold. He managed to open one eye. White. Everything around him was white, even in the dark. And it was cold. So cold.

"That oughta cool him off. Stop his big mouth," one of the men said, guffawing. Luther thought he recognized it as the voice of one of the men who'd killed his father.

Then he knew why the man was laughing. They had taken him far from the mine, up into the mountains. And dumped him in the snow, in the dead of winter, wearing just a torn shirt and pants, and light boots.

They were leaving him to freeze to death.

CHAPTER
SIX

Warm. So warm. He'd heard an old-timer say that you felt warm when you were freezing to death. But why that smell, a musty, ripe smell? And that sound . . . like crackling flames?

Luther opened his eyes, expecting white, finding instead shadows leaping on dark walls. He tried to turn his body, winced from pain, and found that his movements were restricted. He looked down. A huge buffalo robe covered him. That was the smell, the robe. God, it stank.

"Well, by God," a voice said. "Finally showin' a little life."

Luther twisted his head to the side. A man was leaning over him. Beard. Lots of beard and hair. All of it gray. Two bright blue eyes squinted at him from a weathered face. The man smelled a lot like the buffalo robe. For a moment Luther wondered if Fife's company goons had come back for him, taken him someplace . . . But why?

He looked past the man. He was inside a building. A cabin of some kind. The walls were of heavy logs. The flickering light came from a fireplace. "Where . . . ?" he started to say.

"Take it easy, kid," the man said, leaning back away from him. "Found you in the snow, all busted up. Brought you here, stuck you in that old robe to heat up a bit. You was just about gone."

"And who . . . ?"

Luther's head began to swim. So hard to talk, to concentrate. He began to be aware of how much he hurt. His whole body hurt. He drew in a breath, then winced. His ribs . . . he thought he felt them grating. They must be broken.

44

"Don't you worry none 'bout who I am," the man said. Luther realized he was speaking softly. Or as softly as he could; he seemed to have a naturally robust voice. "Jus' you git back to sleep. Rest up. Wait for your strength to find out just where the hell it's gone to, boy."

Safe. You're safe, was what the voice was really saying. Luther let his breath out in a long sigh. Relaxed. Felt sleep coming to take him away.

When Luther awoke again, his head felt better. At least on the inside. No more dizziness. But on the outside it felt awful. He reached up, suppressing a groan as battered muscles complained. His face was swollen, his eyes half-shut, his lips puffed and split. He felt his nose. It was swollen too, but nothing grated; it didn't seem to be broken.

Then he remembered where he was. His eyes tracked around the cabin, looking for the man. No one there. He started to sit up, and this time he did groan. His ribs seemed to be sticking broken ends right through his side. He fell back, groaned once more, then tried again, much more cautiously, and finally managed to sit up, hardly daring to breathe as his ribs adjusted to the new position. Only then did Luther realize that he was naked beneath the buffalo robe. Where were his clothes?

Then he saw them, hanging on a line near the fire, just the pants and shirt, both torn, with bloodstains visible, but obviously washed.

It took him five minutes to move over to his clothes and take them off the line. Another five minutes to pull them on. One of his legs felt like it was broken; he could barely put his weight on it. His knuckles were skinned. He remembered, then, the few good punches he'd managed to land before he'd gone down.

Boots. Where were his boots? Looking around the cabin, he saw them near the fireplace. He hobbled over, picked them up. He knew he'd have to sit down again to pull them on. He managed to sit on the bed, even managed to bend forward, his ribs screaming agony, but he could not pull on the boots. They must have shrunk from the heat of the fire, and he simply could not pull hard enough.

He was gasping for breath, little shallow breaths, working around the pain in his ribs, when the cabin door opened, and the man with the beard and hair came in. "Well," he boomed. "Looky here. Damned if it ain't up an' movin' around."

Luther saw that the man was carrying something. A bloody haunch of venison. He put it down on the cabin floor, came over toward Luther. "You figurin' on takin' a hike, boy?" he asked.

Luther wearily shook his head. "Just . . . wanted my clothes on."

"Well, they're on. Don't need no boots just yet. Plenty warm in here."

Luther agreed with a nodding of his head. Which hurt. He remained sitting on the edge of the bed, afraid to lie down. The man sat on a rickety wooden chair that was obviously handmade. "How'd you git out in the snow, boy, all busted up that way?" he asked abruptly.

"Well, I . . ."

Luther hesitated. Maybe if he said too much he'd end up back in Fife's hands. He didn't know this man, didn't know what connections he might have. The man seemed to read his thoughts. "The name's Jedadiah, boy," he said. When he saw that Luther was waiting for more, he grinned. "Had another name once, a tail on my handle. But I'll be damned if I kin remember it."

He shrugged. "I ain't got no truck with whoever worked you over, for the simple reason that I ain't go no truck with anybody at all. Been livin' up in these here mountains for nigh onto forty years."

His brow wrinkled. He stared off into space. "Or maybe it's more like fifty."

He snorted. "Don't make no mind, it's been a long time. What I'm tryin' to say, boy, is you ain't got nothin' to worry about from me. Lessen you're a lawyer, a preacher, or a goddamned Pinkerton. Varmints like that I shoot on sight. But I would kinda like to know where you come from, just in case anybody shows up, sudden-like, alookin'."

So Luther told him. At first he intended to mention only the trouble with Fife. But eventually, as the memories battered at him, it all came pouring out: his mother's death, the trip West, the banker in Nebraska, the crooked sheriff, his father's activities at the mine, and finally, his father's murder.

During the recitation Jedadiah sat stone still. When it was over, he nodded once. "Yep," he muttered. "Guess the world out there ain't changed much since I last seen it. That old greed, it gits into everything. Turns men crazy mean."

He scratched his head. "I seen that mine. Wandered over that way a year or two back. How anybody could take that purty little valley, an' . . ."

His voice trailed away. "Don't much care for the kinda man who'd do a thing like that. After murderin' that valley, don't come as much of a surprise that he'd murder any man who stood up to him. An' then leave a boy out in the snow to die."

"He'll pay," Luther murmured. He wondered why he hadn't started crying when he'd told it all. Then he realized he'd probably never cry again. "I told him he'd pay, and I meant it."

Jedadiah shook his head hard, as if trying to shake something from it. "What you gotta do now, boy," he snorted gruffly, "is get well. Mend yourself. Then you kin start thinkin' 'bout settlin' accounts. Then, not now. Just so's you remember one thing. The only real account a feller's gotta settle is the account with himself. The rest o' that goddamned, bloodsuckin' world out there, that world o' men, hell . . . it ain't worth a minute of a man's time."

He got up, went over to the door, threw it open. Through it, Luther could see a snowy field, and beyond, the base of a heavily wooded mountain. "I'll tell you what counts, boy," he said, and now his voice was genuinely soft. He tapped his chest. "What's in here."

Then he flung an arm in a broad gesture toward what Luther could see of the outdoors. "An' most of all, what's out there. That's all we really got, boy. An' ain't we lucky we got it?"

CHAPTER
SEVEN

The cuts and bruises on Luther's face healed first. Then the ribs, which were only badly bruised. It turned out that his leg was not broken either, and being young, within two weeks he was back to normal.

He had been wondering, as he healed, where he would go if old Jedadiah turned him out once he was in good shape. By his own admission Jedadiah was a loner, had been living a solitary life up in these mountains for years.

But the old mountain man showed no indication that he wanted him to go. Indeed, after all those years alone, Jedadiah was obviously delighted with the boy's company. "Ain't had a chance to talk like this for years," he told Luther one day. "Seen a lot o' things, learned a little, but ain't had nobody to share it with."

He talked by the hour, his voice slowly losing its harshness, becoming more normal. He told Luther tales about the old days in the mountains, about the trappers and hunters, the explorers, the soldiers and Indians. To Luther this was better than any Ned Buntline novel. Jedadiah had really *been* there, had actually seen the things Buntline only guessed at. He'd done them himself.

"Now that Jed Smith, he made me proud to have the same first name," Jedadiah told him one day. "That old boy was at home in any wild place. He was the firstest white man to see a lot o' this Western country. Why, I remember when he come back from the Yellowstone. Nobody'd believe him at first, all that stuff about hot water shootin' up outta the ground, and the other things he seen there. But he did see 'em, and old Jed never lied. . . ."

Jedadiah scratched his chin a moment. "Well, maybe he'd kinda yarn a little. Hell, we all done that. After spendin' a year or two alone up in these mountains, trappin' beaver, well, hell, when we'd get together in the spring to sell the pelts an' swap stories, yarnin' felt good. . . .

"Now, damn it, what the hell was I jawin' about 'fore I lost the trail? Yeah. Old Jed Smith. He went out to Californy back when it was Spanish. Them Spanish, they was gonna lock him up for trespassin', but nobody was about to git away with lockin' up Jed Smith. He just kinda slipped away in another direction."

When Luther asked him about Kit Carson, a name he'd grown up hearing, Jedadiah scowled. "Never did cotton much to Kit. He's the one left Grizzly Joe to die after that bear half et him. But ol' Joe, he *crawled* a coupla hundred miles, killed him a few Injuns along the way. Woulda killed Kit, too, but figured he was just a stupid kid."

Jedadiah turned his head and spat into the fireplace. "But what bothered me the most about Kit was that Californy thing. When we stole the place from the Spaniards. Kit butchered a passel o' peaceful Injuns, when he was playing soldier against the Californios. Wanted a big name, Kit did. But as far as I'm concerned, he got hisself a bad name."

By now, when he wasn't listening to tales, Luther was helping with the chores, splitting kindling, or dressing out some of the game Jedadiah brought back. Finally, when his leg was completely sound again, the old man took him hunting. Luther was feeling full of life again, but Jedadiah walked him into the ground. Once, when Luther was struggling through a snowdrift, Jedadiah looked back, pursed his lips, and said, "Boy . . . you make more noise than a pregnant moose."

Not Jedadiah. He ghosted along soundlessly, seemingly tireless. Luther did his best to imitate the old man's movements, and was finally able to move with a little more grace and silence. Then, the final stalk, trailing along after a big buck deer. The animal kept appearing, disappearing, and reappearing, slipping from one clump of cover to another. Jedadiah, anticipating the buck's probable direction, led them around in a big circle. A moment later the deer appeared, perhaps three hundred yards away, stepping out of a stand of leafless alder. Luther watched as Jedadiah raised the rear sight on his old Sharps, put the butt against his shoulder, aimed for what seemed only a second or two, then the rifle roared, and a huge plume of white smoke shot out several yards from the barrel.

When the smoke cleared, Luther saw that the deer was down. Jedadiah wasn't even looking in that direction, he was busy reloading the Sharps. Jedadiah noticed that Luther was watching him. "You always reload, boy. First off. Ain't nothin' more dangerous than an unloaded gun."

A few days later, when they were out in front of the cabin dressing some meat, Jedadiah picked up the Sharps and handed it to Luther. "You know how to shoot, boy?"

"Some," Luther admitted, a little smugly, reaching out for the rifle.

"Glad to hear that," Jedadiah said rather drily. "Supposin' you take a shot at that dead limb over there."

Luther nodded, raised the rifle, started to aim. Jedadiah pushed the barrel up. "Not that one. Too easy. The one over there."

Luther followed Jedadiah's pointing finger. At first he thought he was pointing at the air, then he saw, maybe four hundred yards away, a crooked piece of limb sticking up at a forty-five degree angle from an old snag. "Way out there?" he blurted.

Jedadiah spat on the snow. "Sure 'nuff, boy. This old Sharps, she ain't a close-up gun."

Luther went through the motions, aimed high, fired. Nothing happened. He didn't even see where the bullet hit. But Jedadiah, watching the hillside behind the snag, saw snow fly. "Way too low."

He spent an hour teaching Luther how to estimate distance, then flip up the rear sight and set the crossbar for that distance. He taught him how to use the set trigger, so that the main trigger would go off crisply, with a light touch. He taught him how to control his breathing, so that the rifle did not waver, and to fire between heartbeats for the same reason. At the end of the hour Luther had hit the branch twice, cutting off half its length. He felt great pride when Jedadiah finally nodded. "I think mebbe you got the makin's of a marksman in you, son."

Son. The first time he'd been called that since his father had been murdered. Luther felt himself start to choke up, but, after a silent struggle, mastered himself. As he was certain Jedadiah would want him to.

Weeks went by. Jedadiah and Luther spent most of their time out in the mountains, Jedadiah teaching, Luther learning. The heart of the lessons was to cooperate with nature, rather than dominate it. "If you don't get greedy, boy," Jedadiah told him, "if you don't use it all up too fast, if you learn its ways and play by its rules, well, this old world will take care o' you. It'll eat you in the end, o' course, but what the hell . . . fair's fair; you been eatin' it. Them Injuns, they was the ones knew how to live up here in these mountains. Ever'thing I know, I guess I learned from watchin' them."

One day, as if to drive home this lesson, they came upon the camp of some meat hunters. Luther was unprepared for what he saw; it was a little like seeing Duncan Fife's mine for the first time. Desolation. Destruction. Bones everywhere. Stacks of antlers. Rotting hides. Piles of offal.

The hunters were not in the camp. Jedadiah and Luther walked through it, the boy stunned, Jedadiah angry. "Lot of 'em are city fellers from back East," Jedadiah muttered from between clenched teeth. "Wanta come out here and make money off the land. They shoot meat for the railroads, for the town restaurants, for the army. A few more years o' this kinda slaughter, an' there won't be any meat left for honest men who want to *live* up here."

Jedadiah systematically wrecked the camp. But he was not satisfied. "The kinda money these yahoos make, they'll just buy more gear an' come on back. Think I'll hafta palaver with 'em."

Jedadiah led the way down the trail. "They should pass by 'bout here," he muttered. As usual, he had an old percussion Remington .44 stuck in his belt. Luther had never seen him fire it. Now he pulled it out and handed it to Luther. "You take this . . ." Jedadiah started to say. But after watching the way Luther was handling the pistol, he sighed, and took it back. "Maybe you better stick with the rifle. I know you can shoot that."

He grew more serious. "Now listen. Maybe I shouldn't be gettin' ya inta this, but I figure you're just as ticked off about them meat hunters as I am. What we're gonna do is kinda surprise 'em. Have us a little talk. Convince 'em this ain't the place for 'em to be. The trouble is, they might wanta argue."

He looked intently at Luther. "If they get ornery enough, if they go for their iron, you figure you can pull the trigger on 'em, boy?"

A kaleidoscope of images shot through Luther's brain. The banker, the sheriff, Duncan Fife. These meat hunters were of the same stripe. Greedy men who preyed on the world. Without hesitation, his eyes hard, he nodded sharply. Jedadiah smiled. "By God, boy, I think you'll do just fine."

They ambushed the meat hunters as they made their way back to the camp. There were three of them. They were laden with game, with their rifles in scabbards on the back of pack animals. Jedadiah stepped out of the brush, the Remington pointed in the general direction of the hunters. "Hold up, fellers. End o' the road."

The meat hunters froze in place. "Is this a robbery?" one blurted.

"No," Jedadiah said coldly. "It's the end of a robbery. The end of you robbin' these mountains."

The man who'd spoken stiffened. His hand drifted toward the butt of a pistol that was jutting from a holster. As he'd been instructed, Luther, who was back about twenty yards, partially concealed, cranked back the hammer on the Sharps. Clank-clunk! The sound was very loud against the stillness of the snow-covered landscape. The man with the pistol froze, probably wondering how many men were hidden in the brush.

Jedadiah quickly disarmed the hunters. Then he dumped their packs from the packhorses. The hunters were growing more and more angry, but, disarmed, their anger was useless. Luther, watching, saw that two of them did look like city men, out West for a few months of plundering the wilderness. The third man was older, perhaps nearly as old as Jedadiah, dressed like a mountain man, but with a furtive look about him. "You ain't gonna get away with this, Jedadiah," he snarled.

Jedadiah gave the man a long hard look. "Whipple . . . I known you for 'bout twenty years. Ain't never liked you, don't like you now. An' you've known me for that same twenty years. So you know that if you come against me, they'll be carryin' you out feetfirst. The only thing keeps me from ventilatin' you right now for bringin' these bastards up here is that you ain't worth the lead. But if I see you around here again, I may change my mind."

They sent the meat hunters back down the trail, riding bareback on their pack animals, without their weapons, which Jedadiah had broken into pieces in front of them. "Just so's they can't say it's a robbery," he later explained to Luther. "I figure they ain't gonna want to talk about this, anyhow. They'd be lookin' pretty bad."

When they had returned to the cabin, Jedadiah looked troubled. "You ain't never had much truck with pistols, have you?" he asked.

Luther shook his head. "Well," Jedadiah continued, obviously ill at ease, "maybe it's time you learned to use one. On the other hand, maybe you'd be better off if you never did learn. Getting good with a handgun has done funny things to a lot o' men."

He turned away, picked up the pistol from where it was lying on a stump. "Hell, you'll give it a try someday, anyhow. Might as well learn to do it right."

But he did not immediately hand the pistol to Luther, as he had earlier handed him the rifle. "A pistol's not much good over maybe fifteen or twenty yards," he explained. "Not if you kin git your hands on a rifle. Most pistol fights take place up real close, maybe just a few feet separatin' two scared, crazy men. Hell, one time I seen two hombres empty their pistols at each other at ten feet, and miss every shot, just ajerkin' an' apullin' like mad, pistol barrels wobblin' all over the place. You gotta be steady, not lose control even when lead's whistlin' all around you. That's even more important than bein' a good shot."

The lesson proceeded. Jedadiah, seeming not to aim at all, emptied the pistol at a chunk of wood sitting about twenty feet away. Two of the shots missed, but the other three sent the wood skittering this way and that.

"You gotta know how to load it," Jedadiah said. "A misfire is real embarrassin' when somebody's trying to collect your scalp."

He showed Luther how to measure the powder into each of the cylinder's chambers in the shortest possible time, but with the greatest possible accuracy. "You want every shot to be the same," he insisted. "A good eye don't help you none if the bullet don't go where you aim it."

He showed Luther how to press the percussion caps onto the nipples at the back of the cylinder, so that they would not fall off, and just as important, so that they would not let moisture into the chamber, wetting the powder. Finally, he had Luther cap the end of each cylinder with thick grease, so that the flame from one cylinder would not ignite the adjoining cylinders. "Kicks like a mule," Jedadiah said, grinning, "when two or three of 'em go off at once. Kin take a finger right off."

They loaded only five cylinders, leaving the one under the hammer empty. "When I know I'm goin' into a tight spot," Jedadiah said, "I load up all six, an' put the hammer down between cylinders. There's still some chance of a cylinder goin' off, but that extra bullet can really come in handy. Save your life."

Finally, it was firing time. With the pistol held way out in front of him in his right hand, the way Luther had seen it done in so many illustrations of Western gunfights, he began firing at the same chunk of wood Jedadiah had tormented earlier. He even hit it twice, but most of his shots went wide.

"You're jerkin' that thing all over the place," Jedadiah said. "Every time you cock it, you're way off target. Here . . . try this."

He showed Luther a two-handed grip. "It don't look real pretty, like them soldiers do it at their pistol matches, but when the chips are down, son, all you wanna do is be the one who walks away, pretty or not."

Luther found his shooting improved considerably with the two-handed grip. He liked the solid feel of the pistol bucking against his joined palms. He liked the smell of the gun smoke, the feeling of being able to reach way out there and make things happen.

Jedadiah showed him a variation on the two-handed grip. "You hear a lot of crap about people fannin' a pistol," he said. "Fannin' just scatters lead you may be needin' later. Best to do it this way."

He had Luther hold the pistol in both hands, right index finger holding the trigger back, while his left thumb worked the hammer. Luther found he was able to hose bullets out the barrel with considerable control. "For close up only," Jedadiah warned him. "When you wanta knock a man right off his feet."

They fired another half hour, until the pistol, caked with powder residue, began to seize up. Then Luther was given a lesson in cleaning. "Water'll melt away the powder," Jedadiah told him. "But it rusts the metal . . . unless you use real hot water."

Luther washed the barrel and cylinders out with boiling water, the water heating the metal so that it dried easily. Then Jedadiah had him take the pistol apart, to see how it worked. Finally, Jedadiah had him oil each part. "If you use too much oil, it gunks everything up," Luther was warned. "Too little, an' you get rust."

When they were finally finished, with the pistol oiled and gleaming, Jedadiah, smiling, pointed at Luther. "Now, you," he said.

When Luther didn't understand, Jedadiah produced a fragment of mirror. Holding the mirror in his hand, Luther saw that his face had been blackened by powder blowing back out the nipples. The skin around his eyes was the only white part left.

So he washed. And he practiced, day after day, until the Remington felt like an extension of his hands, his whole body.

Finally, one day, when he could hit a piece of hide nailed to a tree thirty feet away, ten times out of ten, Jedadiah walked up to him and took the hot pistol out of his hand. He looked down at the pistol first, then at Luther. "You got the skill, boy. Comes natural to you. And I think you got the guts and the heart. The question is, do you have the brains?"

"What do you mean?" Luther asked, slightly insulted.

Jedadiah let a short silence pass. "What I'm talkin' about is killin', boy. Killin' men. That rifle o' mine, it kin kill men, but it's really made for killin' game . . . buffler, deer, bear. Not this here pistol. It was made for one thing . . . killin' men. Killin' 'em close up."

He looked Luther straight in the eye. "I've killed my share o' men. But not to prove anything, or for the hell of it. Only when it was me or them. Killin's a heavy load to hang on a man. On a good man."

He looked at the pistol again. "You're good with this, boy. Don't let it go to your head."

Luther knew that was about as emotional a statement as he'd ever get out of Jedadiah.

CHAPTER EIGHT

Winter began to lose its hold. The snow grew rotten, then melted, until only patches of dirty gray slush were left. The earliest of the spring flowers thrust up through spongy soil. It was much easier to move through the mountains now; Luther and Jedadiah spent more and more time away from the cabin. Luther continued to learn, Jedadiah to teach, although Luther soon surpassed Jedadiah in his skill with weapons. "You got the touch, boy," Jedadiah said grudgingly. "You could hit a gnat in the ass at a hundred yards. Trouble is, you just about shot up all our powder and ball. We're gonna have ta go in ta town an' git us some more."

"But I haven't got any money," Luther blurted, chagrined that he had so thoughtlessly used up the old man's supplies.

"Don't make no mind," Jedadiah said. "I got me plenty."

"You?" Luther asked, amazed.

Jedadiah smiled. "Guess you thought I was just an old bum. Naw. I got gold here. Wanna see?"

Jedadiah led a dubious Luther into the cabin. "Lotta people keep their stash under a loose board in the floor," Jedadiah said, chuckling. "Don't work here. No boards."

True. The floor was of earth packed as hard as iron. But, way back in a corner, Jedadiah moved a packing crate that served as a cupboard, and under it was a hole in the floor, and in that hole was a terra-cotta jar.

Jedadiah lifted out the jar and set it on the floor. Inside, Luther could see what looked like leather. Jedadiah lifted out several crude leather bags. They chinked pleasantly when he put them down. The old man picked up one of the bags and dumped its contents onto the floor . . . a stream of glittering coins. "Went out to Californy back around '50," he said. "That gold rush thing. Didn't get rich, but didn't lose nothin' either. Brought back around ten thousand dollars worth o' gold, some in coin. This one bag's the only coins I got left. The other bags are nuggets or flakes. I figure there's three or four thousand dollars worth here. Should be enough to buy a little powder and shot."

He smiled at Luther. "An' maybe one o' those newfangled Colts you been tellin' me about."

Luther felt acutely embarrassed. He'd told Jedadiah about the new army model revolver that Colt was bringing out. A pistol that fired metallic cartridges. Quick to load, less likely to suffer a misfire. He'd heard about them while he was still at the mine. After so much practice with the Remington, he'd wondered how they'd shoot, if they'd be as accurate.

"Aw, Jedadiah," he protested. "You can't go and do that. Heck, I been living off you long enough as it is. I . . . feel like I'm not pulling my weight around here."

Jedadiah looked genuinely surprised. "Not pullin' your weight? Hell, boy, you're startin' to bring in more game than me. Pretty soon I can just sit back an' enjoy life, while you do all the work."

"But," Luther continued, "this is your place. Just 'cause you found me in the snow . . ."

"Enough o' this kinda talk," Jedadiah said, a little snappishly. "Ya know . . . there's certain tribes o' people, in certain parts o' the world, that believe if'n you save someone's life, then you're responsible for 'em from then on. Mebbe that's the way I feel. Now, as for that there Colt, what the Sam Hill makes you think it's for you? I been around guns all my life, boy. Long enough to know that it pays to have the best, the most advanced. Hell, when I was a kid like you there was some old codgers still runnin' around with flintlocks. Made it all the easier for them redskins to lift their hair."

Which pretty much closed the discussion. Luther wanted to say more, but decided not to. Maybe Jedadiah was growing lonely in his old age. Maybe he really was enjoying the company, the companionship, that had grown up between them. Luther knew how much he himself liked being around Jedadiah. But he also realized that he was still young, and the more he learned about the great West that lay all around him, the more he wanted to go out on his own, to see more of it.

But he couldn't. Not now. He had nothing. The clothes he'd been wearing when Fife's men dumped him in the snowbank had been replaced by some of Jedadiah's clothing. He had no money, no weapons, no horse. Even his boots had rotted away, replaced by soft doeskin moccasins Jedadiah had made for him by hand.

Yet he would have to go someday. He knew that, and he knew that Jedadiah knew it. But there was no hurry. The mountains were blooming with Spring life, there was game to bring in, and it had finally been agreed that in a week's time they would go into the nearest town for supplies, a journey of several days.

The men arrived the day before Jedadiah and Luther were due to leave. Jedadiah was aware of them first. A bird called. A moment later a squirrel began to chatter angrily. Jedadiah raised his head. Luther was only a couple of seconds behind him. Jedadiah looked over at him, nodded. "Good," he said. "Always keep your eyes peeled and your ears alistenin'. You'll live longer."

There were four of them, mounted. They came riding into the clearing that surrounded the cabin. By now Jedadiah was leaning against the door frame, with the Remington thrust into his belt, while Luther was several feet away, holding the Sharps.

The men came to a halt a few yards away. Luther noticed that none of them were young, although all were considerably younger than Jedadiah. One moved his horse out in front of the others. He grinned. In Luther's opinion, the grin had little warmth in it. "Well, I'll be damned," the man said. "If it ain't old Jed Bass hisself. They said you was somewhere up in these mountains."

Jedadiah's face showed no signs of recognition. "Do I know you, mister?"

The man looked disappointed. "You don't remember me, Jed? Tom Logan. We was out in California together."

Another moment's hesitation, then Jedadiah finally nodded recognition. "Yeah," Jedadiah said. "When we was up around Oroville. Hell, I thought they hung you."

"Nope. Not yet." Logan waved a hand toward the others. "You probably remember Jason Stark, here. He was in California, too. These other fellows, you wouldn't know."

Jedadiah still remained standing by the door. Logan shifted his weight in the saddle. "Ain't you gonna invite us to git down for a spell?"

When Jedadiah continued to hesitate, Logan leaned back, laid a hand on his saddlebags. "Got us some real whiskey. Thought we'd all share it. For old times' sake."

Logan was still smiling. His mouth, that is, not his eyes. Luther realized he distrusted the man. But now Jedadiah began to smile, too. Perhaps it was the offer of whiskey. Perhaps it was simple frontier hospitality. Or maybe he really did want to talk over the old California days with Logan. "Sure, Logan. Take the weight off those nags. We'll set here in front, on the porch. Cabin's kinda small inside."

The men got down. From the stiffness of their movements, they must have been riding quite a while. Jedadiah rolled some cut sections of log up onto the porch, to use as seats. The men sat around in a circle. Logan had produced his bottle. The cork came out with a loud pop. A moment later the bottle was making the rounds.

Luther remained standing to one side, holding the barrel of the Sharps, with the butt resting on his foot. One of the men noticed him standing there, raised the bottle, beckoned him over.

"He don't drink," Jedadiah said curtly.

Luther wondered what had made Jedadiah say that. How did he know if he drank or not? Neither of them had been around alcohol since Jedadiah had found him in the snow.

Logan looked over at Luther, grinned. He turned back toward Jedadiah. "The way he hangs onto that rifle, I figure you musta hired yourself a bodyguard. Gettin' old, Jed?"

Jedadiah had the bottle. He took a hefty swig, wiped his mouth, then passed the bottle along. "Could be," he grunted. "Could be. He sure as hell can shoot."

Logan looked at Luther sharply. Almost with hostility. Why? Luther wondered. Then Logan turned back toward Jedadiah, and started talking about California again. He seemed to know the place well.

Luther continued to stand to one side. As the whiskey passed around, tongues began to loosen even further. Pretty soon the talk was all about the gold rush days. Logan and Stark and Jedadiah did most of the talking. The other two men only put in their oar from time to time. Luther had names to hang on them now. Jim Harrington and Bill Devane. To Luther, they were shifty-looking men. Logan and Stark had something of the mountain man about them. Devane and Harrington reminded Luther of the men in that town where the crooked sheriff had robbed him and his father.

The bottle ran dry. Logan produced another from his saddle-bags, smaller this time, and passed it to Jedadiah. Luther had already noticed that Jedadiah was getting the lion's share of the whiskey. Then Jedadiah looked up, caught him watching. A brief smile flickered over the old mountain man's face. "Luther," he said. "We're gonna need us some meat. All this booze is makin' me hungry. Maybe you kin go out an' bag us somethin' tasty."

"Now?" Luther asked. Since they were leaving tomorrow, they'd let their larder dwindle down to nothing. If he got a big deer they'd never be able to eat it all, not even with Logan and the others here to help out.

"Yep," Jedadiah said curtly. "Now."

Luther did not reply. Jedadiah had never before spoken to him with such sharpness. Maybe it was the whiskey, maybe it was memories of the old days. Stung, he nodded back just as curtly, picked up the pouch containing powder and shot for the Sharps, then walked away toward the edge of clearing. He looked back once. Jedadiah and the four men were still sitting on their cut stump ends, laughing and yarning, and finishing off the whiskey.

It took him only half an hour to find the trail of a deer. He tracked along cautiously, trying to figure out where the deer might be headed. He was totally concentrating on his hunting, when, from the direction of the cabin, which was about half a mile away, he heard a sudden burst of shooting.

He froze. What could be happening? It did not sound like target practice; several of the shots had overlapped, as if a number of people were shooting at once. Something was wrong. Very wrong. He had not liked those men, had suspected that Jedadiah did not like them, either. Yet Jedadiah had . . .

Abandoning the deer's trail, Luther began to run back toward the cabin. The going was difficult. Although the cabin was not that far in a straight line, there were few straight lines in these mountains. The journey took Luther almost fifteen minutes. He was still a couple of minutes away from the cabin when he heard one more shot.

He put on a burst of speed. He could hear horses neighing ahead. He came in sight of the cabin. Logan and two of the other men were already mounted, and riding out of the clearing, leading a riderless horse. Where was the other man? Where was Jedadiah?

Then Luther saw someone lying on the porch in front of the cabin. He called out. The three mounted men saw him, slammed spurs against their horses' sides, made for the tree line. Luther wasted another second staring at the body on the porch, then raised the Sharps, sighted, fired. One of the men—he thought it was the one called Harrington—yelped, reeled in the saddle, but managed to hold his seat. A moment later the three of them had vanished into the trees.

Luther started forward. Then he remembered what Jedadiah had told him. About empty guns. If he ran toward the cabin the men might come riding back out, and with the Sharps empty they'd have an easy time killing him. He flipped open the Sharps' breech, rammed in a paper cartridge, then slammed the breech shut. The sharp back edge of the closing breech cut into the cartridge, spilling powder into the chamber.

Luther was already running as he pressed a copper percussion cap onto the rifle's nipple. He glanced over toward the place where the men had vanished into the trees. Nothing showed. He jumped up onto the porch . . . and nearly tripped over a body. A quick glance told him it was Devane. Jedadiah lay several feet away, half-propped up against the wall. The Remington lay a yard from his right hand.

Luther knelt. "Jedadiah," he half-whispered. He did not expect an answer; the entire front of Jedadiah's body was drenched in blood. Luther could see bullet holes.

Jedadiah's eyes flickered open. With great difficulty, they focused on Luther. "What . . ." he murmured. "What are you doin' back here, boy?"

He turned his head, grimaced with pain. "You gotta watch out!" he said, with more force. "They'll back shoot ya. . . ."

"They're gone," Luther replied. "I don't think they'll be back. I hit one of them."

A moment's incomprehension, then a slow smile appeared on Jedadiah's face. "I tried to warn the bastards. Told 'em you were a good shot. Thought that might o' . . ."

His voice cut off as a grimace of pain twisted his features. Blood trickled from his mouth. Luther dropped the Sharps, moved closer, helped lower Jedadiah's upper body until he was lying flat. He thought for a moment that Jedadiah had died; nothing seemed to be moving. Then the old man's eyes flickered open again. "Hadda get you outta the way."

Jedadiah's voice was so low that Luther could hardly understand the words. "I figured they was up to no good. I was right. They was after the gold. Logan knew I took a fair chunk outta

California with me. Guess he heard I still had some."

"They came here to rob you?"

"Yeah. Worked out that way. I saw it comin', yanked out the .44, got Devane. But the rest of 'em got me. Musta hit me . . ."

He stopped talking for a moment, his chest heaving. It was obviously costing him a lot to talk. "That last one Logan put inta me, just before they lit out. Hurt the worst. They was lousy shots, but he took his time with that one. They had the gold by then. I wanted 'em gone before you got back. Those treacherous bastards wouldn't think nothin' o' shootin' a boy. . . ."

Suddenly his whole body stiffened. More blood poured from his mouth. Then he lay still. My God, he's dead! Luther thought again. But, as before, Jedadiah's eyes opened. "Glad you hit one of 'em," he muttered. He barely had the strength left to speak.

Luther bent closer, talking, his voice hard. "I want you to hear this, Jedadiah. You said they'd shoot a boy. Well, maybe I'm not such a boy anymore. I'm going after them. I'm going to run them down. I'm going to find them and kill them. For you, Jedadiah."

Jedadiah's eyes refocused on Luther's face. "By God, Luther, I think you might just do that."

He managed a half-smile. "In a way, I kinda feel sorry for 'em. They . . ."

Another wracking spasm. Silence for a moment. Then, a few more words. "Go after 'em, boy. Find the bastards. Close the account. . . ."

A sigh of expiring breath, then, fiercely, "Do it, Luther. Lift their goddamn hair."

CHAPTER NINE

Luther buried Jedadiah on a rise behind the cabin. There'd been so much burying: his mother, his father, now Jedadiah. Was there nothing else to life?

Maybe not. Because there was going to be more burying. Tom Logan. Jim Harrington. Jason Stark. They'd need burying, too, because he was going after them. He was going to keep his promise to Jedadiah.

He didn't bother burying Devane, he simply dragged him to a ravine and tipped him over the edge, food for coyotes, buzzards, or any other varmint that could stomach him.

He debated burning the cabin. Kind of like the Viking funerals he'd read about. But it was a good cabin, built by Jedadiah with real care, and improved over the years. He'd leave it here, have some kind of a place to return to from time to time.

He outfitted himself as well as he could from Jedadiah's belongings. He'd take the Sharps, of course, and the Remington, which Logan and the others had been stupid enough to leave behind. He'd take what powder and shot remained, some clothing, and all the food he could carry. Plus a big old slouch hat he'd seldom seen Jedadiah wear. There was a little money, too. In preparation for the trip to town, Jedadiah had put a few gold coins in his pocket. His killers, their minds filled with vivid imaginings of a hoard of gold hidden somewhere in the cabin, had not thought to search him.

Luther closed the cabin door, slipping a dowel into the big wooden hasp, the closest he could get to locking the place. If some passerby saw fit to use the cabin, that was fair enough.

He set off on foot. For several days he followed the trail Logan and the others had left. Down, always down, out of the mountains, heading toward the east. He found two places where they'd camped for the night. Maybe if he'd left earlier he'd have caught up with them. Unlikely. They were mounted; he was on foot. The camp fires were old, his quarry long gone.

He finally lost their trail where it merged with the trails of other horsemen, wagons, and even a small herd of horses someone must have been taking somewhere. He was in a more settled area now. He passed occasional towns. In one town he used some of his gold to purchase an old horse and a bridle. He didn't figure he had money enough for a saddle.

Now he began his questioning, asking again and again if anyone had seen a particular group of men riding through, one perhaps wounded. Sometimes the replies he received sent him off rapidly in this direction or that. Some of the leads were wild-goose chases, and he had to return to the last point where he'd had definite sightings and start out again.

More days passed. Then weeks. Luther became known in the area, a tall young man—a new, grim set to his features forestalled most people from thinking of him as a boy—always asking after three men, named Logan, Stark, and Harrington. Finally, he got a real lead. Information about a man who'd been laid up in a town about three days away, recovering from a gunshot wound. A man who fit Harrington's description.

Luther hurried his pace, although his horse was beginning to pull up lame. He wished he could buy a better animal, but he intended to hang onto what little money he had left; the chase might prove to be a long one. Perhaps he'd need money for train fares.

When Luther reached the town, he started asking his usual questions. He struck pay dirt almost immediately. "Jim Harrington?" one man said. "Sure. He's been livin' over at the hotel ever since Doc patched him up."

Luther picked up the Sharps and immediately started toward the hotel; he could see it down at the end of the street, a wobbly, two-story affair, built of weathered clapboard. Then he hesitated, remembering something Jedadiah had taught him. He stepped behind a building, and quickly loaded the Remington's single empty chamber. That extra shot might count. Shoving the Remington back into his waistband, he started toward the hotel again, looking up at the windows as he approached, wondering if Harrington was behind one of them now, watching him come closer, lining up his sights.

He made it to the door without any trouble, then went inside, into a narrow hallway. Tight quarters for the Sharps. He leaned it against the wall, then continued on down the hallway. A door opened. Luther's hand reached down for the butt of the Remington. "Did I hear somebody come in?" a voice called out. Luther did not think it sounded like Harrington's voice. He let his hand drift away from the gun butt.

A moment later a cadaverously thin man stepped out into the hallway. He gave a little start when he saw Luther. "Oh! Thought I heard somethin'."

His eyes passed quickly over Luther, assessing his possibilities as a financial asset. Apparently, he reached an unfavorable conclusion. "Rooms here cost fifty cents a night. In advance."

"I'm not looking for a room," Luther replied.

"Well, then. . . ." The man started to turn away. A dismissal.

"I'm looking for a man. Name of Jim Harrington. I've been told he's staying here."

The man's eyes shifted back toward Luther. "Who told you that?"

"A man down the street."

The man looked Luther over again. "Well, maybe he is staying here, maybe he isn't."

Luther looked around quickly. Standing here, talking in a hallway, using names, could alert Harrington. He might be listening right now. He might come out of a doorway at any moment, shooting.

Luther took a step closer to the man, until their faces were only a couple of feet apart. He looked the other man straight in the eye. "Is he here, or isn't he?" he demanded, his voice hard now.

Caught by the intensity of Luther's gaze, the man started to say something, hesitated, swallowed nervously. Those eyes. . . . Ice, chips of cold blue ice. For the first time, fear clawed at the man's belly. "He, uh . . . yeah, he lives here."

"Which room?"

The question was like a whip crack. Already Luther was looking away, glancing up and down the hallway, and at the stairs at the end.

The man felt a moment's relief. Then Luther's eyes were pinning him again. "But he ain't here now!" the man said quickly. "He went out to eat. At the restaurant. He ain't been a well man.

Somebody shot him. He . . ." Suddenly it occurred to the man who might have shot Jim Harrington. His voice trailed away.

"Does he have a gun?" Luther asked.

"Yeah. He always . . ."

"Good."

Luther turned away, started down the hallway toward the front door. Suddenly he stopped, turned back to face the man. "You stay here," he said, his voice low, but not pleasant. "If I see you out in the street . . ."

The man shook his head violently. Luther, picking up the Sharps on his way to the door, turned his back fully and walked outside.

He had not bothered to ask the man where the restaurant was. It was a very small town, just one street. He'd already seen what looked like a restaurant about halfway down the street. He walked toward it, the Sharps held loosely in his right hand. If Harrington came out now, and started shooting, he'd pick him off with the rifle.

But Harrington did not come out. Luther walked right up to the restaurant's front door. Once again he let go of the Sharps, resting it next to the doorjamb. Opening the door, he stepped inside.

The restaurant was larger than he had expected, maybe twenty feet by twenty, with a scattering of sagging plank tables. Through a door in the back wall, Luther could make out a kitchen. He'd already seen Harrington, seated at one of the tables, leaning back in his chair, an empty plate in front of him. There was only one other man inside, bent over a plate of what looked like stew. A clatter of pots was coming from the kitchen.

Harrington looked up, his gaze passing lightly over Luther. He started to look away, unconcerned. Maybe it was something about the way Luther was standing, facing him squarely, looking straight at him, that made Harrington look again. For one long frozen moment, the two men remained staring at one another, Luther's gaze steady, Harrington's eyes widening in slow recognition.

"I've come for you, Harrington," Luther said, his voice flat and deadly. "I promised Jedadiah."

"Son of a bitch!" Harrington snarled. He was already getting to his feet, reaching for the butt of a pistol that rode high on his right hip. Later, Luther was not able to remember his own initial movements; it was simply trained reaction, the result of all those hours spent with the Remington. Which was now in his right hand, the fingers of his left hand closing over the fingers of his right, his left thumb fanning back the hammer, his right index finger holding the trigger all the way back.

Harrington got off the first shot. Luther was vaguely aware of something hot passing close by his face. Then the Remington began to roar, the shots coming so fast that they blended into one another, a continuous thunderclap of sound.

Luther missed with the first shot, but his steady, two-handed grip made a slight correction, and the next four shots slammed into Harrington's body, driving him backward. Harrington's pistol fired one more time, discharging a wild shot into the floor.

Then it was over, perhaps four seconds after it started, with Harrington lying on his back on the floor, and Luther still standing, with the Remington held out in front of him. A huge cloud of blue-white gun smoke hung in the room. The man at the other table sat frozen, with his fork halfway to his mouth. Now, belatedly, he uttered an oath, and dived for the floor. Luther, hearing the sudden sound, spun, his pistol tracking. The man on the floor held out his hands to show that he had no weapon. Relaxing, Luther turned back toward where Harrington lay.

He was still alive, moaning, writhing a little. Luther walked over to him, looked down. Harrington was literally shot to pieces. As Jedadiah had been. Luther felt a moment's nausea, fought it down. He got down on one knee, bending over the wounded man. "Harrington," he said, "can you hear me?"

Harrington's eyes were huge with . . . with what? Pain? Fear? His eyes managed to focus on Luther. "You," he muttered. "A kid. Who woulda thought . . . ?"

"The others!" Luther snapped. "Where are they?"

"Huh?"

"Logan. Stark. Where are they? I want them, too!"

Understanding flickered in Harrington's eyes. He started to laugh, but the laugh turned into a whine of pain. "Ah, Jesus," he whimpered. "It hurts."

"The others!" Luther repeated, more savagely this time. He raised the pistol, as if he were going to fire into Harrington's body again, although he knew he would not be able to.

Harrington didn't know that. "Ah, Jesus," he pleaded. "For God's sake, don't shoot me no more!"

Then he began to babble. "You're welcome to 'em. The bastards. . . ." And now his voice grew bitter. "They left me here on my own, 'cause I couldn't travel fast enough. We'd heard somebody was on our trail. They lit out, left me here with some old sawbones who could hardly crawl outta the bottle long enough to . . ."

"Where'd they go?" Almost a shout now.

A slow shake of Harrington's head. "Oh, God, I don't know. Just lit out."

Seeing the rage in Luther's eyes, he hastily added, "I think I remember Tom, he was sayin' somethin' 'bout headin' north, maybe toward the Dakotas."

Luther fought to calm himself. He knew he was unlikely to get much more from Harrington. He looked around quickly. The other man was still on the floor, careful not to move. A face appeared in the kitchen door, a woman's face, then dodged back out of sight.

Harrington was now talking in a monotone. "That ass Tom Logan an' his big ideas. Told the rest of us that the old geezer had took him a fortune outta California almost thirty years ago, an' had it all socked away in some cabin."

A choking sob, either from pain or self-pity. "Warn't nothin' there but maybe three thousand dollars worth o' gold. A thousand dollars a man. Small pickin's. . . . They give me the smallest share, a few hundred in gold coins. Then lit out on me. . . ."

A crafty look came into Harrington's eyes. "If you leave me alone, don't hurt me no more, I'll give you the money. It's in my room, under the mattress . . . what's left of it. You get that old sawbones over here, let him patch me up again, then you kin have the gold. Ever' blessed bit of it. I . . ."

Harrington's voice had been growing fainter and fainter. Now it stopped altogether. Luther saw that Harrington's eyes, while still open, were staring into nothingness. His chest, which had been heaving with pain, was no longer moving.

Luther stood up. He was suddenly aware that only one load remained in the Remington. He reached into his pocket, pulled out a spare cylinder that he kept there carefully wrapped in a cloth. He removed the cylinder pin from beneath the Remington's barrel, tipped the old cylinder out, slid the new one into place, then rammed the pin back. He checked all the caps, to make certain none had fallen off the nipples.

"Can I get up, now?"

For one wild second Luther thought it was Harrington. But it was the man on the floor. Luther nodded curtly. The man stood up, automatically brushing at his clothing. "I heard everything he told you," the man said. "About robbing somebody. About giving you the gold. And," he added, "he did draw first."

A witness. Luther hoped he'd stick with his story. He looked back to where Harrington lay, in a huge, still-spreading pool of blood, then he nodded at his witness and walked out of the restaurant.

He remembered to pick up the Sharps from where it lay against the door frame. Then he headed down the street, in the direction of the hotel. And as he walked, he was aware that something had changed. Something inside him. He felt different. Altered.

Then it hit him . . . how he'd been changed. And he realized the change would be fundamental. Permanent.

He'd just killed his first man.

CHAPTER
TEN

The gold was where Harrington had said it would be, under the mattress. Just a small leather bag. Not much to show for the lives of three men. As Luther walked out of Harrington's room, the thin man he'd talked to before, probably the hotel's owner, stuck his head out of a doorway. When he saw Luther, he ducked back inside. He'd heard the gunfire, wasn't about to interfere.

Walking back to his horse, Luther thrust the sack of gold coins inside his shirt, mounted, and rode out of town, his tired old nag sighing resignedly. Some getaway, Luther thought wryly. He was damned lucky there was no posse after him.

That night he camped out on the trail. He ignored the gold until the next morning, then opened the bag and counted the coins. There was a little more than five hundred dollars, counting what he already had. In a sense, spoils of war. In the little war between himself and Harrington, Luther had definitely been the winner. He could have probably taken Harrington's horse and equipment, as well as the gold. But that would have been plundering. He didn't think he was ready for plundering. Not yet.

Sliding up bareback onto the old horse, Luther rode on. Around midday he saw a town in the distance. He caught himself hesitating before he rode in. It occurred to him that this new cautiousness was a part of the change he'd felt come over him after killing Harrington.

But he finally did ride in, and in the town be bought a good horse and saddle, along with saddlebags, and a rifle scabbard for the Sharps. Plus a new pair of boots, and trousers, and shirts without holes. Plus one other purchase. He was walking by a hardware store when he noticed a pistol on display in the front window. From pictures he'd seen, he knew it was one of the new cartridge Colts.

He went inside. A few minutes later the Colt was in his hand. It felt lighter than the Remington, maybe it was because the Colt didn't need a ramrod assembly. He spun the cylinder, pulled back the hammer, tried the trigger . . . and absolutely fell in love with the pistol. It had wonderful balance, felt right in his hand. And, with its case-hardened frame, and blued-steel barrel and cylinder, the Colt seemed downright beautiful.

The store's owner was at first dubious of Luther, but when Luther pulled out the leather bag to buy the Colt, and the man heard the chink of gold coins, he immediately trotted out all his sales skills. So Luther found himself buying not only the pistol, but a holster complete with cartridge belt, a cleaning kit, and two hundred rounds of ammunition.

Luther was so anxious to try out his new purchases, which had used up half his money, that he decided not to spend the night in the town, although he could now afford a hotel. First, there was the new horse to get used to. He'd bought a big black mare, which had not been ridden for some time. As soon as Luther swung up into the saddle, before he'd had time to seat himself properly, the mare bucked him off into the dirt. Luther, angered, immediately picked himself up and started back toward the horse. Then he stopped, froze in place. Gingerly, he checked his pistol. Other than having dirt ground into what had been a shiny new holster, the pistol was undamaged.

So he remounted, wary this time, and managed to ride out the mare's bucking, which was only halfhearted, anyhow; she seemed to kind of like her new owner. Within a few minutes horse and rider were trotting out of town, with Luther testing the horse's mouth, and the horse testing how much it could get away with. Not much, she finally decided.

For the first time since he'd hit the trail, Luther made a relatively comfortable camp. Happy with all his other sales, the man at the hardware store had thrown in a bedroll at a reasonable price. So Luther slept well, alert, however, to his horse's condition, waking from time to time during the night to make certain the mare had not pulled the lead rope free from the tree where Luther had tied it.

In the morning Luther took out his new pistol, swabbed excess oil out of the barrel, then loaded the cylinder with six rounds. He

liked the way they simply slid in through the loading gate. Before
he closed the gate, he spun the cylinder, admiring the shine of
clean new brass.

After checking the horse's lead rope again, he started to walk
away from the camp. Then hesitated. Finally, he picked up the
Sharps and took it with him. Jedadiah had told him repeatedly
of the folly of separating yourself from your weapons. "A dumb
thing like that could just as easy end up separatin' a fella from
his hair," the old mountain man had warned gruffly.

Luther had noticed a whitish patch on the trunk of a tree, about
forty yards from the camp. He moved to within thirty feet of the
tree, raised the Colt, cranked back the hammer, and let fly. Blam!
A good solid recoil. Maybe a little heavier than the Remington;
the Colt was in .45 caliber, and the bullet seated in the cartridge
case was conical, rather than spherical. A lot more weight of lead,
with a corresponding kick.

And steady as a rock. Each bullet was stable, each load fairly
accurate. A nice gun to shoot.

Luther had been watching the mare out of the corner of his
eye. With the first shot the mare jerked her head up and reared.
Her nervousness continued for a while, but by the time Luther
had fired thirty or forty rounds, the horse had settled down.

He moved closer to the horse, picking a new target. Closer
and closer, until he was standing only six feet from the mare,
firing. The horse obviously didn't like all the noise, but remained
fairly calm.

Pleased with the pistol, Luther spent the next fifteen minutes
cleaning it. Then he saddled up and rode north of east, the direction in which he suspected Tom Logan and Jason Stark might be
headed.

Now he began to have doubts. He remembered how hard
Harrington had died. Did he want to see other men die that way?
Would revenge harm him in some manner? His father had often
talked to him about such things, about a man becoming blinded
by passions, hardened by violence. Luther had kept at least part
of his word to Jedadiah; he'd tracked down one of his killers.
Maybe he should just ride on, enjoy his new horse and gun, and
try to find a life for himself. He was young, he was . . .

Not a coward. Not a welsher, and he'd promised Jedadiah.
Promised Fife, too, that he would pay for his father's death.
But, more important even than that, than promises, than pride,
there was something larger at stake. Men like Logan, Stark, and

Fife should not be able to destroy the lives of other men and walk
away free. It had to be made right! Somehow, the scales had to
balance, or the world would be a place of insupportable horror.
The abuses of evil men should be confronted . . . and punished.
And Luther, in his youth, living in the midst of an illusion of
personal immortality, could think of no better agenda for his
own life.

So he rode on. Once again he began stopping at towns, asking
about two men, Jason Stark and Tom Logan. He got answers;
they'd been seen here, they'd been seen there. A trail began to
emerge, heading always northeast. Perhaps too definite a trail, but
Luther was unaware of this, unaware that news of his quest, along
with news of the death of Jim Harrington, had spread over quite a
distance. Far enough so that, in some of the places where Logan
and Stark stopped to spend the money they'd stolen from Jedadiah
Bass, the story reached their ears. And they acted, setting a trail
that could be followed, but a trail that they could control.

One day, about a month after the gunfight with Harrington,
Luther was nearing a small town out on the prairie. Perhaps he
would rest here for the night, then continue on the next morning.
He had information that suggested Stark and Logan were holed
up in another town, about a day's ride ahead. Funny how the
information had been coming in, people almost volunteering it,
some of them people Luther would have thought more likely to
keep their mouths shut. Like those two shifty-looking drunks a
few days back who'd told him about a town where they were sure
two men who sounded like Stark and Logan were spending time.
And money.

So, the trail was probably coming to an end. At least, where
Jedadiah's killers were concerned. In a couple of days either
they'd be dead, or Luther would. Not that Luther really imagined
he could be killed. Not after the success of his encounter with
Harrington.

Still, as Luther neared the town where he intended to spend the
night, there was just the slightest tickle of unease at the back of
his mind. After all the weeks of fruitless searching, the path had
become so clear. Almost as if it had been laid out for him. He
was at the edge of the town now; it was just a small place, with
the usual cluster of weathered plank buildings in the center, plus
a scattering of houses spreading outward until there was nothing
left but prairie. It was a little bigger than some of the towns he'd
seen lately, maybe four or five hundred people. A big enough

town so that he couldn't see all of the buildings at once.

Something made him slow down as he rode in, some inner voice, that tickle of unease. Funny, it was early afternoon, and there was no one in sight. Then he noticed a man in work clothes, walking out of what looked like a saloon. Probably with a few drinks in him. The man stepped out onto the boardwalk, stretched, and seemed about ready to turn to his right.

Then he saw Luther. And froze in place, staring. A moment later the man ducked back into the saloon.

Luther reacted immediately, which was the only thing that saved his life. A livery stable lay to his left, a good-sized building with big double doors. Which were open at the moment. Luther rode straight for that doorway, and had almost reached it when Tom Logan and Jason Stark, having waited all day, having set up this meeting as best they could, stepped out into the open, pistols in their hands.

"Damn you, kid!" Stark shouted. If he hadn't wasted the time, if he'd fired before he'd shouted, it might have ended right there. He was standing a little in front of Logan, which slowed the other man a little, and by the time Stark got off his first shot, Luther was moving so fast he was hard to hit.

Luther rode straight in through the stable doors, with lead flying all around him. His mare, shaking with fright, skidded to a stop inches from a line of stalls. Luther slid out of the saddle and jerked his Colt from its holster.

Just in time. Logan and Stark were rushing the doorway. They saw him at about the same time he saw them, and all three opened fire. But Luther was in partial darkness, hard to see, and he was firing fast, his bullets driving the two killers away from the door and back outside.

Then the hammer of Luther's Colt came down on an empty cylinder. He felt sick to his stomach as he heard the dull thud of firing pin against expended primer.

Logan heard it, too. "His gun's empty!" Logan shouted. "Come on, Jason! Let's finish him off!"

They came in through the doorway again, while Luther was fumbling in his saddlebags for the Remington. As Luther worked the .44 clear, Logan was already firing. One shot missed, but the other slammed into Luther's side. He felt himself spin, start to go down, but managed to stay on his feet by holding onto the low side of a stall with his left hand. Now the .44 was up, and he was firing, one-handed, driven by panic, his shots missing, but the smoke and flame spurting from the Remington's muzzle, at a time when his attackers had expected him to be holding only an empty pistol, drove them both back out the doorway.

"Jesus!" Stark shouted, ducking around the corner.

Luther knew he had, at most, one shot left in the Remington. He'd dropped the Colt, could see it lying six feet away. He knew that if he bent down for it, either Logan, or Stark, or both, were likely to stick their heads around the corner of the doorway and fill him full of lead.

Shoving the Remington into his waistband, he started over toward his horse, which was prancing nervously. But he had to stop for a moment, as a bolt of pain shot through his side. God, he'd forgotten about being hit, but he had to make it to the horse before she completely spooked. Gritting his teeth, he staggered over to the mare, which was as appalled by the smell of Luther's blood as she had been by the thunder of gunfire.

But Luther's training of the horse, his familiarizing her with gunfire, a lesson repeated many times over the past few weeks, paid off. The horse stood, shivering, as Luther jerked the Sharps from its saddle scabbard. What really saved him was that Logan and Stark had both taken time to reload their pistols. Luther could hear them muttering from their cover just the other side of the stable's big doorway. Perhaps they felt safe there, sure that no pistol bullet could penetrate the stable's thick wooden walls.

But with the Sharps, it was another matter. Propelled by a massive load of powder, the rifle's huge seven hundred grain bullet not only went through the wall, but took out a chunk four inches across, carrying with it stinging splinters of wood. Luther heard a wild yell from someone outside; it sounded like Stark. "Christ! Bullet took off part o' my ear! What the hell kinda arsenal does that kid have in there?"

Figuring he'd gained a few minutes, Luther led his horse around behind the stalls. On the way he retrieved the Colt, and as he staggered along he furiously shucked out empties and replaced them with fresh loads. It was hard to do—he was half bent over because of the pain in his wounded side—but he made it all the way to a pile of thick hay bales, behind which he hid himself, accompanied by all three guns and his saddlebags with their load of ammunition.

Now it became a siege. Logan and Stark, having recovered their courage, had now, with great caution, remembering the power of the Sharps, moved around to the side of the building.

They fired, from time to time, through windows, or through the doorways, always on the move, never staying in one place long enough for Luther to have a good shot at them with the Sharps. He did manage to get one more shot out of the rifle, with the same damaging effect on the stable's walls, but this time without coming anywhere near his attackers.

But at the same time they could not come anywhere near Luther. The piled up hay bales, with Luther in the center, soaked up bullets effortlessly. To actually reach him, Logan and Stark would have to cross a lot of open space. And by now they'd come to respect the accuracy of Luther's shooting. Just as Jedadiah had warned them . . . before they killed him.

Luther's problem was time. He'd pulled a spare shirt out of his saddlebags and wadded it up against the wound in his side, but he was still losing blood. And beginning to feel slightly faint. He knew that if he lost enough blood, he'd pass out. Then they'd simply come in and finish him off. ·

It was Logan and Stark who gave up first. The shooting had gone on too long. So far, they'd managed to buffalo the town, but they had to consider that someone might have gone for the law, or perhaps the local citizens would find their courage and do something about stopping all this shooting. It was during a lull in the firing that Luther heard somebody, probably Logan, mutter, "Come on. Let's make tracks. We'll git the bastard another time."

Luther, slowly reloading the Remington, gritted his teeth against the pain . . . and against becoming overconfident. Maybe Logan's words were just a trick to smoke him out. He remained in his little fort even after he was sure he heard the beat of hooves—it sounded like two horses—start up a short distance away, then diminish rapidly.

Perhaps ten minutes passed. Luther kept busy, checking to make sure that all his weapons were loaded. Suddenly, he stiffened. He heard footsteps just outside the stable doors. He raised the Sharps, ready to send another round through the wall.

Then a voice called out, "Hey! You in there! Those other two fellas lit out. No reason for you to stay holed up."

Luther hesitated. It certainly didn't sound like either Logan or Stark. But, they could easily have somebody helping them, trying to get him to leave cover.

"We're sick o' you people shootin' up our town," the voice continued. "We just want you to get the hell outta here."

It was possible, Luther thought. Just possibly true. But did he have any choice? If he stayed here much longer, he would probably bleed to death. Better to make his move now, while he had some strength left.

Getting to his feet was more difficult than he'd expected. So was the trip to his horse. He thought he'd never get the Sharps into its scabbard. Swinging up into the saddle took three tries, but he finally got mounted. He rode straight toward the stable doors, his left hand holding the reins, his right hand holding the Colt. Cocked.

There were several men outside. Some held guns, others appeared to be unarmed. He saw several women peering out of doorways and windows. One of the men stepped forward. He jerked his chin in the direction of Luther's Colt. "You won't need that. We just want you to get the hell outta here."

"I'll put my pistol away when all of you put your guns down," Luther said, his voice grating with pain.

The man shrugged. His pistol was still in its holster. He turned around to face the other men. "Fair's fair," he told them. "Put 'em away, boys. We sure as hell don't want no more shootin'."

Luther didn't relax until he was the only one left with a gun in his hand. The men stepped back, opening up a path for him. They could go for their guns again, but he doubted any would. The man, the one who seemed to be speaking for the rest, turned to face Luther again. "Just ride on," he said curtly. "And don't come back."

Luther nodded, managed to stuff the Colt back in its holster. He swayed in the saddle. Suddenly, someone else was speaking. It was a woman's voice, sounding light and clear after the man's voice. Or was Luther just imagining it? Sound seemed to be receding; he felt as if he were stuck right in the center of a huge batch of cotton wool. "How can you ask him to leave?" Luther heard the woman call out. "Can't you see he's wounded? Can't you see he's just a boy?"

The spokesman snorted. "As far as I'm concerned, anybody packin' that many guns ain't no boy. He's dangerous. He's gotta be run out. . . ."

"Oh, is that so?" the woman asked derisively. "I didn't see any of you big heroes running those two gunmen out of town, even though they were braggin' all over the place about waiting here to ambush someone. And that's just what they did. I saw it start—they opened up on him without warning. You were scared of them, and the only reason you're acting so brave now is that the odds are down to one wounded boy against a whole town."

There was grumbling from the men, but also a few shamed faces, then another woman, watching from a doorway, called out shrilly, "You jezebel!" Her voice was an ugly shriek. "You'd be just the one to stick up for some dirty stranger! For anybody wearing pants!"

The woman colored, looked angry, started to speak, but was drowned out by catcalls.

"Don't worry about it, lady," Luther said, surprised how weak his voice sounded. "I plan on riding out, anyhow."

He kneed his horse into motion, turning in the saddle to face the woman. "But, thanks . . . for what you said."

God, but it was hard to sit the saddle. He was vaguely aware of the woman speaking again, not to him, but to the others. "Oh, you God-fearing, kindly, good samaritans," she said acidly. "Letting this boy—"

Again a shrill cry from one of the women. "You shut up, Kathy Jackson. If our men had any gumption, they'd run you outta town, too. Why we women put up with . . . ."

More words, some shouted, some muttered, most of them becoming jumbled up in Luther's mind. The people he was passing had faded to vague shadows. It was growing dark. Strange, he had thought it was only a little past midday, with bright sun. But dark. So dark.

He was vaguely aware of someone calling out. He thought it sounded like the woman who had stuck up for him. Then, there was a sense of falling, of not knowing which way was up, which was down. Something struck his body a blow, a heavy thud. Had he hit the ground?

There was light above him again. He opened his eyes and was immediately blinded by the sun, which seemed to be hovering directly in front of his face. He could vaguely make out a silhouette, dark against the sunlight, hear a voice murmuring something, the words unintelligible, but the tone soothing, warm.

Then . . . total darkness.

CHAPTER ELEVEN

Swimming up from a great depth, no sense at all of time passing. The last thing Luther had seen was a face hovering over him. As his eyes opened, the face was still there. A face he could see more clearly now. "What . . . ?" he murmured. The word came out as a croak. His tongue felt huge in his mouth, dry, useless.

"You're awake!" An exclamation of delight from the woman. "I was wondering. . . ."

Luther started to sit up, but could not. He was too weak. And his side hurt. "What . . . ?" he managed to say again, then could not find it in him to force any more words past that swollen tongue.

"Just rest," the woman said. "You've been wounded. You lost a lot of blood. I wasn't sure if you'd ever . . . Well, it's good to see you awake."

That voice . . . he was pretty sure it belonged to the woman who had defended him from the townspeople. He wanted to talk, he had questions . . . if he could manage to stay awake. A massive lethargy was sweeping over him. The woman's voice was so calm, so soothing. He was vaguely aware that he was in a bed. Inside a small room. There were curtains on the windows. Curtains like the ones his mother used to be so proud of. Good. If there were curtains, it must be all right. Safe to trust this woman, just lie back, not fight the lethargy, rest. . . .

The next time he woke up, his sense of time had returned. He knew that he had been sleeping for quite a while. His eyes opened more easily, and his mouth was not so dry. But the woman was not there. Awakening, he had expected to see her face over his own, as before. But there was no one in the room except himself.

Just as well. Time to figure out where the hell he was. He studied the room more carefully. It was smallish, curtains and all. Quite clean. The bed was comfortable, although he realized that he ached from having lain in it for so long. How long? he wondered. He moved, caught his breath as pain shot through his left side, where the bullet had hit him. He ran his right hand over his torso, discovered that he was naked underneath the blankets, except for a wide bandage wrapped all the way around his ribs.

Footsteps, coming his way from another room. Luther tensed; nothing makes a man jumpier than being hurt. It could be Logan or Stark. He instinctively looked around for his weapons. There they were, the pistol belt hanging from a wall peg next to his clothing, his rifle leaning upright in the corner.

But the footsteps were light and quick. A woman's step. A moment later she came into the room, saw him watching her, and smiled. "Well, you're starting to look like a human being again. Just barely."

She came over to the bed, sat down in a chair that had been positioned just a couple of feet away. "How are you feeling?" she asked.

"Well . . . okay, I guess."

He spoke absently, using most of his attention to study the woman. He decided that she was nice-looking, in kind of a mature way. Maybe the same age as his mother had been when she'd died. Thirty, thirty-five. Real mature. With thick dark hair and pleasant features. Probably not really beautiful, not like some of the women he'd seen in books and magazines. Not like an actress, or somebody like that.

What he really liked about the woman was her expression. Alert, thoughtful, alive. No hardness about her at all. "Can you tell me about . . . ?" he started to say, passing his hand over the bandages.

She looked down at his body. Suddenly he was terribly aware of being naked under the blankets. "You were shot in the side," she said. "But you were lucky. The bullet passed right on through, probably bouncing off a rib. I say lucky, because there are no real doctors around here, there would have been nobody to do a decent job of digging out a bullet."

"So then," Luther asked, "who . . . ?"

"I patched you up. Cleaned out the wound, dug out any pieces of your shirt that might have got forced into it, then poured whiskey right into the hole."

She smiled. "You were lucky you'd passed out. It would have hurt. Then I cleaned up the rest of you, wrapped those bandages all around your ribs, and let you sleep."

Cleaned him up. Bandaged him. Once again Luther was uncomfortably aware of being naked. She hadn't mentioned having any help. She must have . . .

She read his unease. "That's what women are for," she said. Luther looked at her sharply. Had he detected just a hint of bitterness in her voice?

He ceased to worry about that particular problem when she asked if he was hungry. Hungry? His stomach felt like it had shrunk to the size of a walnut. Within ten minutes he was spooning down hot, delicious stew, amazed to discover that he couldn't eat very much of it. Maybe his stomach really had shrunk down to walnut size.

A half hour later he was asleep again. "Get your rest," the woman said as his eyes began to flutter. "You did lose an awful lot of blood. You've got to build it back up."

The routine was set for the next few days: eat and sleep, eat and sleep. Finally, four days later, stiff and sore from lying in bed for so long, Luther swung his legs over the side, and planted his feet on the floor. The woman was out of the house, buying something. Maybe some more meat to cram down his throat. It took him so long to gather the strength to get out of bed that he was afraid she'd return before he was able to dress himself. As it was, he only managed to get his pants on; with his stiff side, putting on his shirt proved to be too damned painful.

The woman came back half an hour later, to find him sitting gingerly, half-dressed, in a chair in the living room. She seemed startled at first, then smiled. "Getting ready to saddle up and ride out?" she asked. The words were cheerful enough, but he thought he detected just a trace of alarm in their tone.

He knew her name, had first heard it from one of the women who'd been screaming at her in the street. Kathy Jackson. He'd started by calling her Mrs. Jackson. She'd corrected that to plain Kathy. "And it's Miss Jackson, anyhow," she said, just a little primly. Miss? he wondered. How could a woman that old not be married?

They'd talked a little, during the days when he'd been building up the strength to get out of bed. Not much had been said. He had mentioned, once, that he'd been nursed back to health by an old mountain man, pretty much like she was doing. "Oh?" she'd replied. "Where is he now?"

"He's dead."

The words came out flat and hard. Kathy looked surprised.

"The men who shot me," Luther said. "They robbed and killed him."

Kathy nodded slowly. "And that's why you were after them."

"Uh-huh. I'd already caught up to another of them. He's dead now. I thought I had those two. But I was stupid. Careless."

"How old are you, Luther?" she asked. Pretty much like his mother might have asked.

"Nineteen."

She nodded slowly. "I guess a man grows up quickly out here. Nineteen, and you've already . . ."

She let the rest of the sentence fade away. Luther remembered the feeling that had come over him after he'd killed Harrington. She knew. She knew how he felt. Nineteen, and he'd killed his first man. And was planning to kill more.

They never talked of it again, and as Luther mended, he began to discover more about Kathy. "The scarlet woman," she said lightly, when he finally got up the courage to ask about some of the things the townswomen had shouted at her. But her light tone could not completely hide the hurt that he sensed.

"I fell from grace," she explained, her face grave. "My family came to this town when I was sixteen. About a year later I fell in love with a man. Someone just passing through, as I eventually discovered. But I loved him, as much as a girl that age can really love anyone, and he convinced me that he loved me, too. One thing led to another, and all of sudden I was, well, in the family way. Hell, let's call a spade a spade. I was pregnant."

Luther was slightly shocked. Not because of the facts she was detailing, but because he'd seldom heard a real lady say "hell." Or use the word, "pregnant." Most women wouldn't even talk about their arms and legs. Those were "limbs." Like a tree. Not part of a body, a flesh and blood body prone to sin.

"Being pregnant wasn't such a disaster in itself," Kathy continued. "It happens, out here, where everybody is a long way from a preacher. But when I began talking about marriage, the father-to-be's feet started moving, and I never saw him again."

A long silence followed. Kathy was looking down at the floor. She murmured something under her breath. He thought she'd said something like, "the bastard," but he couldn't be sure. She finally looked up. "The scandal nearly killed my parents. Actually, I think it did. They died just a year later, one after the other. They were good to me, though. Refused to send me away. Took care of me all through the pregnancy. In a way, they were looking forward to the baby, their first and only grandchild. I had no brothers or sisters."

Another long silence. Finally Luther had to ask. "And the baby?"

Kathy looked up. Straight at him. Her face was void of any expression as she replied, flatly, "It died. At birth. I think that was the final blow for my parents. All that scandal and shame, and nothing to show for it."

They never again discussed this particular subject. But bit by bit Luther learned more about Kathy Jackson. When he asked her why she hadn't simply left the area, her answer was simple. "And how would I live? I may be an outcast here, but I do survive. My parents left me the house we lived in, plus a smaller house. This one. I rented out the big house and moved over here. I just manage to get by."

One night, Luther found Kathy drinking a bottle of wine. The bottle was nearly empty. She began to talk about herself, told him that she was indeed an outcast. No decent man would marry her. Not that she would marry any of the oafs around here, anyhow. But she did have natural desires. That was how she put it. Natural desires. She didn't really elaborate, but Luther got the impression that, from time to time, some of the local men paid her little visits. And left her little "gifts" that made it possible for her to survive with a bit more comfort.

She did have one dream. "San Francisco," she told him one day, when he was almost well. "I've always wanted to go to San Francisco. Live by the ocean. It's supposed to be such a civilized town, but still Western. I could never live back East."

When he asked her why she just didn't sell up, take the money, and head out to San Francisco, she laughed. "With the money I could get for these houses, in this poverty-stricken hole, I'd last about a month in San Francisco. No, Luther, it's just a dream."

She had other, lesser dreams, most of them revolving around literature, art, and music. Which was one of the reasons she wanted to go to a sophisticated city like San Francisco. There were many books in the house. She encouraged Luther to read them. When he did, avidly, losing himself in Sir Walter Scott and Dickens, she asked why he did not go back to school, get himself an education. "You could work your way through," she insisted. "You could make something of yourself."

He smiled. She was beginning to sound like his father. Then his smile faded. "I have a few things to do first," he said coldly.

She nodded, sighed. "Yes. The great male myth of revenge . . . manliness. Which is very likely to get you killed, Luther."

Luther stayed with Kathy almost a month. Toward the end, she was tutoring him in Latin. A frustrated schoolteacher, he figured. Once again, kind of like his father. Too bad his father and Kathy couldn't have met. Too bad. . . . No, it was better not to think about maybes.

Luther and Kathy became close friends. Cut off from the outside world, they shared interests in reading and travel, although Kathy had done no travelling at all. She was enthralled by the tales Luther told her about his and his father's odyssey. She introduced him to books he had never read before. Strange, he thought one day, secretly studying Kathy from across the room as she bent over a book. Strange that he could end up feeling so close to somebody so old. Not as if she was a parent, but simply a companion.

Luther began to go out of the house, hoping that walking would build up his strength. The townspeople avoided him. He did not mind; they disgusted him.

One day he was walking by a smithy, and heard the clang of iron against iron. On impulse, he walked inside. The smith was standing over an anvil, hammering away at a length of glowing metal. Luther watched the metal take shape. It looked like it was going to be a knife. A damned big knife.

Finally, the smith looked up. "Something I can do for you, boy?" he asked. His tone was neither friendly, nor unfriendly. Encouraged, Luther pointed down to the cooling metal. "A knife?" he asked.

The man nodded, and now his face took on a little more animation. "Yep. I kinda specialize in knives. Make other stuff, too. I even shoe horses, for eatin' money. But knives are what I like."

"Pretty big blade," Luther opined, to make conversation. Metalworking fascinated him.

The man smiled. He laid down both hammer and metal. "Let me show you some of the knives I've made."

Turning, he started toward a doorway, Luther hesitated, then followed the smith into what looked like a combination living quarters and shop. The man opened a drawer, took out several bundles wrapped in cloth, and laid them on a countertop.

For the next few minutes Luther watched, enthralled, as the smith unrolled one bundle after another, five in all. And inside each bundle was a knife. They weren't just any old knives, but very special ones. Works of art. The smith was beaming now, pleased by Luther's obvious appreciation of his work. Luther turned one knife over in his hand, letting light play along the blade. "How come it has all those wavy lines?" he asked.

"That's what they call a Damascus blade," the smith explained. "You take a piece of metal, fold it over, then beat it out flat while it's still hot. You fold it again and again. That makes lots of layers of metal. Thousands, by the time you've folded it enough."

"Kind of looks like when the light hits silk," Luther said reverently. He had never seen anything quite so beautiful.

"Makes the blade strong," the smith explained. "Strong and flexible. And sharp as hell."

"You got any big ones like this?" Luther asked.

The smith shook his head. "Damascus blades are hard to forge. I just made that little one for the fun of it."

He was watching Luther shrewdly. Finally, Luther spoke. "How much would it cost to make me a big knife, with a Damascus blade? A real fighting knife?"

The smith thought for a moment, and when he finally replied, his voice was firm. "One hundred dollars."

Luther did not haggle. "How soon?" he asked.

The smith smiled. "Give me a week. Maybe ten days."

Now Luther had something to take him out of the house, a definite place to go. Every day he headed for the smithy and watched his knife being made, watched the smith fold and pound the glowing metal, watched the general form of a big blade take shape. The smith seemed pleased that Luther showed so much interest in the process. He explained every step. Luther listened avidly.

Luther had told Kathy about the knife. She seemed amused at first, then strangely sad. "More weapons," she said softly one day. "You have so many already."

"You never have enough," Luther replied. Once again, she looked sad.

One night something happened that Luther had been thinking might happen. He was in bed, half-asleep, when he heard someone enter the room. Kathy—he'd know her step anytime. He did not move. A moment later the blanket was drawn back, and she slipped into bed with him. What followed was like a dream. A warm, sweet dream. Later, as he drifted off to sleep again, he was half-aware of Kathy leaving the bed, moving away. In the morning, as they sat at the breakfast table, Kathy said nothing, just smiled at him. A smile as warm and sweet as what had happened the night before.

She came to his bed again, two nights later. This time, before she left, she said, softly, "I'll miss you, Luther."

"Maybe I won't go," he replied.

"You have to go. You're young, you have those . . . things to do. You can't stay here, and you know it."

True, he did know it. He would go. Kathy would stay. He knew that she was not a particularly adventurous person. She loved her comfort, her books, her quiet life, her dreams about San Francisco. And if she ever did reach San Francisco she would resume, there, the same kind of life—quiet, reflective. So different from the path Luther knew that he must travel.

A day later his knife was finished. Over the past few days he'd watched the smith grind the blade finer and finer, watched the tang take shape. He was amazed by the hours the smith spent just polishing the blade, until it shone like fine watered silk, with wavy lines running its whole length, shifting shape as the light shifted.

Now it was in his hand. It was a huge knife, with a blade a foot long and over three inches wide. "But it's so light!" Luther burst out, surprised by the heft of the weapon.

The smith shook his head. "Not really. It's the balance. I'm glad you noticed."

And he did look pleased, gratified by Luther's obvious delight with the results of his labor. He pointed to the broad hilt. "Brass," he said. "To catch and hold the other man's blade. And look there, at the pommel."

He was pointing to a cone of steel at the butt end of the grip, which protruded past Luther's hand. "You hit somebody over the head with that," the smith said, grinning, "an' he ain't gonna get up."

More directions. "Don't you go grindin' away at the edge with a rough stone," the smith warned him. "You'll ruin the polish, and the edge. Just keep kinda polishin' it with the stuff I'm gonna give you, an' the knife will always be sharp as a razor."

When Luther left the smithy, his new knife rode in a fine leather sheath on his left hip. He proudly showed it to Kathy when he returned to the house. She dutifully exclaimed over its excellence, but he could see the sadness deep in her eyes. For they both knew that the making of the knife had been the only thing keeping him here. He had healed completely; he was ready to hit the trail.

He packed up the next morning. His mare had been in the otherwise empty stable behind the house. The animal was a little fractious as he saddled and bridled her, but it was all show; the mare was as ready for the trail as Luther.

Good-byes were short—a quick embrace in the hallway—and then Luther was outside, swinging up into the saddle. Kathy stayed just inside the doorway, watching as he rode away. He turned once, waved, thought he saw her wave back. He forced himself to look ahead. Leaving was turning out to be a little harder than he'd imagined.

His route took him through the town. He was halfway along the main street when he saw a man step down off the boardwalk. Luther recognized him as the one who'd demanded he leave town, the day of the fight with Logan and Stark. Luther rode straight up to the man, who, finally noticing him, gave a little start of surprise.

Luther stopped his horse a few feet away. Eyes met, Luther sitting high, the other man having to look up. The man was decidedly nervous. "Kathy Jackson," Luther said flatly. "If anybody bothers her, I'll be back."

He turned his horse around the man, watched him step quickly out of the way. Far more than he had to. Luther, glancing to the side, could see fear in the other man's eyes. Justified fear, because Luther knew that if anyone harmed Kathy, he definitely would be back. He owed her. Owed her for more than his life. He'd ridden into this town a boy bent on balancing a wrong. Thanks to her, he was riding out a grown man.

CHAPTER TWELVE

Once free of the town, Luther's regrets over leaving Kathy faded away, replaced with the pleasure of once again being on the trail. It was early fall, the air was crisp and clean, the prairie grasses were golden. Luther felt wonderful. Having very nearly been killed, he was enormously aware of being alive. Colors were more vivid, the smell of the grass sweeter, the light just a little more intense.

From time to time his left hand brushed against the hilt of his new knife. Like a kid with a new toy, he pulled the knife from its sheath. The blade glittered in the bright prairie light as he turned it this way and that. A clump of tall weeds lay ahead. Luther maneuvered his horse in that direction, slashed with the knife, barely felt any resistance as the incredibly sharp edge sliced through the thick stalks.

Luther felt immediate regret. He studied the blade intently, to see if he'd scratched the mirror finish. He sighed with relief when he saw that he hadn't.

He put the knife away. What now? he wondered. Start on the trail of Logan and Stark again? If so, he'd be a lot more careful this time, try not to let them know he was coming.

Then it occurred to Luther that he was only about a two-day ride from the town where his father had opened the hardware store. Which immediately brought to mind Mr. Chase, the crooked banker who had stolen his father's savings. Perhaps it was time to pay Mr. Chase a visit. Settle an old debt.

By late the next afternoon, Luther was only a few miles from Chase's town. He waited until dark before approaching closer.

He guided his horse up a wash, dry at this time of year. When he and his father had lived here—my God, but it seemed like a long time, a lifetime ago—Luther had spent a great deal of time wandering over the prairie. In those days, full of Ned Buntline Westerns, he had practiced slipping along Indian style. He knew the best ways of approaching the town unseen. He was able to approach quite close, right next to Mr. Chase's house. The house was out past the edge of town, on a little rise, with clumps of trees surrounding it. Very private, and, at the moment, in darkness. Luther remembered Mr. Chase as having been a bachelor. Apparently he still was.

Luther tied his horse in a grove of trees behind Chase's barn. Then, on foot, he moved into the town, slipping from building to building, hunting patches of dark shadow. Finally, he was only ten yards from the bank. The bank, like the house, was dark. Closed for the day.

From his place of concealment, Luther could see all the way down the main street. Ten minutes later he saw Chase come out of a restaurant. Luther remembered that it had been Chase's favorite place to eat. Clearly, he still had the same habits as before. Good old Mr. Chase. As regular as a clock.

Luther watched while Chase, as expected, headed for the saloon. Luther remembered his father spending hours in that saloon with Chase, laughing, talking, joking, discussing the issues of the day . . . before Chase had stolen his father's money, foreclosed on the store.

Chase spent two hours in the saloon. When he left, Luther could see that he was weaving slightly. Good, he would not be alert, he would probably sleep like a hog.

Luther followed Chase back to his house, saw a light spill from a window as Chase lit a lamp. The lamp moved from room to room, finally ending up near the rear of the house, where Luther figured the bedrooms were.

The light went out; the entire house was in darkness. Luther let an hour pass, then moved silently toward the house. Before leaving his horse he'd exchanged his boots for the moccasins Jedadiah had made for him. Moving soundlessly, as Jedadiah had taught him to move, he approached the rear door, tried the knob. As he'd expected, it was not locked. Around these parts hardly anyone locked their doors.

Staying close to the walls, to minimize the chance of creaking floorboards, Luther headed toward the room where he'd last seen the light. He was sure he had the right room when he heard loud snoring from behind a partially open door.

He peered inside. A half-moon had risen, its soft glow illuminating the room. It was a bedroom, all right, heavily furnished, with two chests of drawers, a couch, an armchair, end tables, and a large bed. And in that bed was Chase himself, snoring away, one arm flung out to the side.

Luther entered the bedroom, moving more swiftly now. There was only a faint whisper of sound as he slid his new knife from its sheath. He walked right up to the bed, looked down at Chase for a moment. The man's mouth was hanging slack. His face looked more puffy than Luther had remembered.

Chase was not wearing a shirt. Luther laid the cold blade against the upper part of Chase's chest, slid it higher, toward the man's throat. Chase stirred, muttered something in his sleep, refused to wake up. Luther slapped him hard across the face.

"Huh?" Chase burst out, coming awake, starting to lunge upright in the bed, but Luther pressed his left hand against Chase's face, forcing him back down. He held the knife in front of the startled man's face for a moment. Moonlight gleamed off the huge blade. Luther saw Chase's eyes focus on the knife, then widen with shock.

Luther slipped the knife lower, laid the razor edge against Chase's throat. "Move, and I'll cut your head off," Luther said flatly.

Chase had indeed been about to move, to lunge upward again, to fight his attacker. Now he froze in place, aware of the coldness of steel against his skin. "What . . . ?" he blustered. "What the hell do you want?"

"I've come to settle an old account, Chase," Luther replied, his voice still flat and hard. He noticed, then, that Chase's eyes had flicked to one side, and that his right hand was starting to work its way beneath the pillow.

"Uh-uh," Luther snapped, pressing the knife a little harder against Chase's throat. Chase froze in place. Luther could see a thin line of blood begin to well from the side of Chase's neck. Luther thrust his left hand beneath the pillow, felt smooth metal, pulled out a pistol. He tossed the pistol across the room. "Try anything like that again," he said coldly, "and I'll cut your throat right back to your neck bones."

He was aware that Chase did not recognize him. Why should he? The last time Chase had seen him, Luther had been a boy.

"Luther McCall," he said softly. "Come to pay you a visit. Talk over old times."

A moment of incomprehension in Chase's eyes, then awareness. "Horace McCall's boy?" he burst out.

Luther nodded. "I've come back to collect a debt."

The knife pressed harder again. Chase shrank back into the bed. "Oh God!" he whimpered. "Please. . . ."

"What's the matter?" Luther asked. "You don't want to die?"

Chase started to shake his head, but, with the knife pressing so hard against his throat, he thought better of it.

"Pretty silly to die for stealing three thousand dollars, isn't it?" Luther continued. "Normally, that'd only get you a few years in the lockup."

"Please. . . ." Chase whimpered again.

Luther pretended to hesitate. "Maybe you're right," he said thoughtfully. "Maybe I'm overdoing it. Maybe you should just be punished a little."

"Yes," Chase gasped. "Look . . . I can give you back the money. Then we'll be square."

Rage shot through Luther. "You son of a bitch! How the hell can giving me three thousand dollars make it right? My father's dead! Dead because we had to leave here like beggars!"

He suddenly jerked Chase out of bed, then dragged him over to a sideboard. Hauling on his arm, he stretched the arm out straight, so that Chase's right wrist and hand were lying on the sideboard. He raised the big knife high. "I'm not going to kill you, Chase," he snarled. "I'm just going to cut your fingers off, one by one!"

"No!" It came out as a shriek. Chase automatically curled his fingers.

"All right . . . the whole damned hand!" Luther shouted.

With desperate strength, Chase tore away from Luther, backed against a wall. Luther could tell he was about to run. Switching the knife to his left hand, he drew the Colt, pulled back the hammer. "Move, and you're dead," he said coldly.

Perhaps it was because Luther did not yell that Chase obeyed. He froze in place, looking as if he were trying to melt right back into the wall. Luther silently cursed himself. He was handling this badly. Memories, long-suppressed anger, were ruining his concentration. It was tempting to just kill the man. But he had a use for him. I've got to keep cool, he reminded himself. If he'd learned anything from the fiasco with Logan and Stark, it was to keep cool, to plan, to let no one read his intentions.

"Okay, Chase," he finally said, his voice more reasonable now. "I suppose you're right. You pay me the money, and we'll call it quits."

A huge sigh of relief exploded from Chase. "Yes . . . yes! And I'll make it four thousand. Kind of like interest on a loan. Like it was a loan."

Luther nodded. "All right. I'll go along with four thousand. Just hand it over."

As Luther expected, Chase shook his head vigorously. "But . . ." he spluttered. "You can't imagine I have it here? In the house? It's locked up in the bank. In the safe. I'll get it for you first thing in the morning."

Luther laughed bitterly. "Oh, really? Sure. And in the morning, when there are plenty of people around, you'll just tell me to go to hell. Do you think I'm a fool, Chase?"

He raised the pistol. He'd lowered the hammer, now he cocked it again. Chase shrank away from the sound, not knowing Luther had no intention at all of shooting him. Not when things were finally starting to go his way.

Chase took the bait. "Don't!" he wailed, covering his face with his hands. Luther was aiming at his head. "We'll get it now! We'll go to the bank! I can open the safe, take out the money!"

"You're lying!" Luther snarled, suppressing a grin. He wanted very much to get inside that bank, but he did not want to drag an unwilling man with him. He wanted Chase eager to go, eager to cooperate. And, thinking he faced death, Chase was indeed eager.

Chase dressed quickly, after Luther had checked his clothing for weapons. They left the house, slipped quietly through the town, with Luther half a step behind Chase. "Remember," Luther hissed, "if you try and run, I'll use the knife. Hack right through your neck."

But Chase was not about to run. He seemed more afraid of the knife than of the pistol. They reached the back door of the bank without incident. Chase pulled out a key ring, fumbled for a while, finally got the door open. Once inside, Chase led the way directly into the back room, where Luther knew the safe was. They had to light a lamp, which made Luther nervous. What if someone saw the light, grew suspicious, investigated?

After missing the combination once, Chase finally got the safe open. The inside of the safe was stacked with money, some in gold, most in greenbacks. Chase quickly counted out four thousand dollars, started to hand it to Luther. But Luther shook his head. "Uh-uh, Chase. You mentioned interest. But you and me, we have different ideas as to what fair interest might be."

There was a large sack sitting in a corner. Luther picked it up, tossed it to Chase. "Thirty thousand dollars," he said, his voice very hard. "Count it out, and put it in the sack."

Chase's mouth fell open. "But . . . !" he burst out. "You can't be serious! Thirty thousand dollars? That would nearly break the bank!"

"Nearly, but not quite," Luther said coldly. The knife was in his hand again. He placed the point beneath Chase's chin, forced the other man to raise his head high to avoid being cut. "Put it in the bag, Chase."

The two men locked eyes for a few seconds, Chase's eyes desperate, Luther's as cold as ice. And as before, on that day when Luther, only a boy then, had faced Mr. Chase, a grown man, in the street outside the bank, it was Chase who looked away. He was totally beaten, shaken by the cold certainty in Luther's eyes. He knelt, and with shaking hands, began shoveling money into the bag. "No!" Luther snapped. "I want you to count it. Make certain it's only thirty thousand dollars."

Chase, certain the bank was being cleaned out, in effect robbed, looked up in surprise. But when Luther repeated his demand Chase began counting, counted out thirty thousand, five thousand of it in gold, and put it in the sack.

They immediately left the bank and started back toward the house. Chase staggered along as if he were drunk. "I'm ruined," he kept muttering to himself. "I'll never be able to cover it all."

Luther smiled. Just as he'd figured . . . Chase had been stealing from the bank. Once a crook, always a crook. He'd stolen from Luther's father, unreasonable to imagine he wouldn't steal from others. Through the bank, of course. Depositors' money. Which was why Luther had taken only thirty thousand dollars. An even amount. If he'd simply cleaned the bank out, it would be obvious robbery.

They reached the house, went inside. Luther herded Chase into a closet. He expected Chase to become frightened again, but the man was obviously numb, totally beaten. "I'm going to get some rest," Luther told him. "I'll leave just before daylight. If you try to get out of that closet while I'm still here, I'll gut you like a fish."

He closed the door, turned a big old-fashioned key in the lock. It was a flimsy lock; Chase would have no trouble breaking out of the closet if he really wanted to.

An hour passed. Luther, keeping perfectly silent, waited across the room. Finally, the knob on the closet door began to turn, very slowly. Luther bounded across the room, making lots of noise. He banged on the closet door. "Goddamn it, I told you. . . ."

A frightened squeak from inside. "No, no! I just . . ."

Luther let another half hour pass. Then he walked soundlessly into another room. He'd noticed it before, it seemed to be an office. He quickly located paper and ink, sat down and began to write, using big block letters that would be easy to see from a distance. That would attract attention. He wrote a simple message to the effect that an irate customer had discovered that Chase had been embezzling from the bank. That an audit was in order.

He walked back to the closet, making plenty of noise. After rattling the doorknob, he slipped away silently, leaving the house by the back door. His horse was where he had left her, standing asleep. He apologized to the mare for leaving her saddled for so long. The horse snorted. Luther took the snort as an acceptance of his apology. He swung up into the saddle, then rode straight into town.

Not a thing moving, no one in sight. Using a rock, he tacked the notice up onto a high wooden fence right in the middle of town. The fence was often used for public notices. Someone was sure to see it.

After finishing with the notice, Luther sat in the saddle for a moment, looking around the town. Strange, but everything seemed smaller than he remembered. A boy's memories, a man's realities. He turned his horse, and rode out of town, certain that he would never again ride this way.

CHAPTER THIRTEEN

"You're sure she can only get the money if she's in San Francisco?" Luther asked.

The banker spread his hands, a gesture of goodwill that Luther was not sure he trusted. "Of course," the banker reassured him. "Since you've set up the trust that way. She'll have to apply at the office of our San Francisco correspondent personally. Except for the initial travel funds, of course. I'll take care of that; I'll take care of notifying her. And the money will be paid out over time, so much a month, until, after five years, she can withdraw, if she chooses, whatever balance is left."

The banker hesitated. "And you're sure she's not to be notified of where the money came from?"

Luther shook his head vigorously. "She's not to know anything about me at all."

She *would* know, of course. Or at least have a strong suspicion. That didn't matter, just as long as she could never be sure, or her pride might not let her accept the money.

Luther smiled. It was strange to be in a bank, talking to a banker, entrusting him with a great deal of money. However, to accomplish what he wanted to accomplish, he'd had little choice but to work through banks. And this was one of the biggest and most reputable banks in Denver. Well, as reputable as any bank could be. Besides, he thought, smiling again, if they cheated him, he could always come back and rob the place.

He had ridden straight to Denver with the thirty thousand dollars. His object was to use the bulk of the money, twenty-five thousand dollars, to finance Kathy's dream . . . to live in

San Francisco. The banker had shown him how—set up a trust account with Kathy as beneficiary, but only if she actually lived in San Francisco. That should break her inertia, break her free of the town in which she had been buried for so long. If not, well, that was her choice.

The remaining five thousand dollars Luther had determined to keep for himself. For expenses during his hunt for Tom Logan and Jason Stark. One thousand was to go with him in cash. He had a letter of credit from the Denver bank which he was assured would make further funds available whenever he needed them. As long as he was near a bank. He was learning that bankers could be very useful. As long as they didn't decide to steal your money. They had to be watched carefully. To trust a banker's word was to be stupid. Everything had to be signed and witnessed.

Luther left the banker's office feeling that something broken had been made whole again. The money Chase had stolen had been his father's. He knew his father would have approved of helping Kathy.

Now what? He had no idea at all where Logan and Stark might be. Their trail should be very cold by now. He would have to start hunting them all over again. But more carefully this time.

He was thinking about Logan and Stark, remembering the fight at the livery stable, when he realized he was passing a gun shop. A large gun shop. And right in the middle of the display window was one of the new Winchester center-fire rifles.

He walked into the shop and asked the clerk if he could take a look at a Winchester. The clerk hesitated; Luther did not appear to be terribly prosperous, but a long steady look from those cold blue eyes convinced the clerk to be polite. The sales pitch started; this was a big-city gun shop. "We have them in two calibers, sir," the clerk said. " .44-40 and .38-40. Totally new cartridges. A lot more powerful than the old Winchester Yellow Boy .44s." He sniffed. "They were only rimfires."

Luther examined the ammunition first. They were really only pistol cartridges. The bullets were driven by forty grains of powder. A heavy load. He debated for a while over which caliber to choose. With a lighter bullet, the .38-40 would shoot a little flatter. But the .44-40 would pack a heavier wallop.

He settled for the wallop, the .44. Now it was a choice of rifles. The full-length rifle had a twenty-four-inch barrel and held fifteen rounds. The carbine had a twenty-inch barrel with twelve rounds.

He chose the carbine. It had a little less range, but the Sharps would take care of any long-range shooting. He was looking for a gun that would put out a lot of lead, fast, and take men down with more accuracy than he could get from a pistol. If he'd had one of these carbines at the livery stable, he could have shot Logan and Stark to pieces.

Taking his new carbine, along with four hundred rounds of ammunition, Luther returned to his hotel. He made only one more major purchase while he was in Denver. A pair of field glasses.

On the way back to the hotel he bought a newspaper. Lying on his hotel bed, he read it leisurely. Suddenly he burst out laughing. There was a story about a banker over in Nebraska, named Chase, who had been caught embezzling from his depositors. A trial was imminent.

Luther rode out the next morning, his horse groaning under the new load of ammunition. The two rifles, the Sharps and the Winchester, were snug in their saddle scabbards. The load lightened considerably the second day on the trail when Luther started using up some of the .44-40 ammunition, testing his new carbine. First he dismounted and tried it for accuracy, working on the sights with a file and light hammer, until they suited him.

Then he tried rapid fire, shooting from the hip, working the Winchester's loading lever as quickly as he could, sending out a stream of bullets. He cut a small tree right in two, about four feet off the ground. He was impressed.

Next, he mounted his mare, and practiced running his horse flat-out, while he stood in the stirrups, with the reins in his teeth, peppering targets as he raced past. God! If Jedadiah could only see him now!

Satisfied, and with only two hundred rounds of carbine ammunition left, he made camp for the night. He slept well, feeling secure, with the Colt .45 inside his bedroll and the carbine within easy reach.

The next morning, while washing in a stream, he let his mind grapple with some serious decisions. It was time to sort out priorities, weigh options. There was Logan and Stark to consider. And, of course, Duncan Fife. In addition, there was one more loose end that needed tying up. Maybe he should take care of that first.

Now he set out with a purpose, and by the fourth day he was near the town where the sheriff had robbed Luther and his father of their wagon, weapons, and belongings. Instead of riding straight on in, he tied his horse behind a hill several hundred yards from the town, took his new field glasses from his saddlebags, and moved to the top of the hill. Lying concealed behind a bush, he studied the town carefully. It was amazing how the field glasses brought everything so close. He could see the front door of the saloon, thought he recognized a man who came out onto the boardwalk. Although he couldn't be sure. It had been a long time ago.

The town looked the same. Seedy. Run-down. He stiffened slightly when another man came out into the street. It was the sheriff who had robbed them. Good. He was still here.

Luther waited until the sheriff was no longer in sight. Then he returned to his horse. He took off his gun belt, and stuffed it inside the bedroll lashed behind his saddle. He thrust the Colt into the waistband of his trousers, with his shirt concealing the butt. The knife he left in its sheath on his left hip.

Mounting, he rode into town. Right up to the saloon's front door. It was about the same time of day as when he and his father had arrived. He wondered if the same men would be in the saloon.

Some of them were. The first person Luther saw was Snake-Eye, slouched against the bar. Snake-Eye's single orb focused on Luther, then moved away. Luther walked up to the bar. The bartender gave him a quick once-over. Luther saw the man's eyes widen when they lit on the sheaf of bills Luther had shoved into his shirt pocket. The bartender gave an almost imperceptible nod to Snake-Eye and a couple of the other men.

They began to close in while Luther was sipping his drink. Whiskey. He was trying to decide whether or not he liked the taste. Kind of interesting, he decided, as long as you drank it really slow.

Snake-Eye sidled closer, until he was only a yard to Luther's right. Two other men moved in from the left and from behind Luther, cutting him off from the rest of the room. Luther turned to face them. "You yahoos want something?" he asked, in a light, almost amused voice.

That halted them for a moment. Why wasn't this man scared? But Luther could see their eyes focusing on that wad of money in his shirt pocket. "Yeah," one of the men snarled. "We want what you got."

There it was, right out in the open. "Then come and get it," Luther said coldly.

The man who'd spoken moved first. He was big, taller than
Luther, and much heavier. "Smart ass," he grunted, lunging forward, blocking the path of the man with him. Luther had been
leaning back against the bar, apparently wide open to an attack.
The man was already swinging when Luther planted the toe of
his boot right between his attacker's legs. The man let out a wild
yell, half of pain, half of surprise, then bent double, further getting
in the way of the man behind him.

But Luther had no time for either of them. He knew that
Snake-Eye was his greatest danger. Luther was already turning
to his left, while at the same time moving away from the bar. Sure
enough, Snake-Eye was already going for him. He still owned that
Arkansas toothpick; it was in his right hand, driving straight at
Luther's throat.

Luther's hand closed on the grip of his knife, pulled it from
its scabbard. He enlarged the motion into a wide, backhanded
sweep. He felt little resistance as the huge blade cut cleanly
through Snake-Eye's arm, just above the wrist. Snake-Eye froze
for a moment, staring in disbelief at the stump of his arm, then
down at the floor, where his hand lay on a bed of filthy sawdust,
still holding the Arkansas toothpick.

Then Snake-Eye began to scream, a high, ululating wail, a
cry of terror and horror. Holding the stump of his arm, from
which blood was spurting in regular jets, he staggered round and
round in a circle, his mouth open wide, while he screamed and
screamed.

Luther turned. With the knife held out in front of him, a
smear of Snake-Eye's blood red against the bright steel, Luther
approached the remaining two men. The one he'd kicked in the
groin was just beginning to recover. The other was backing away
quickly. Luther caught sight of another man, getting up from a
table near a side wall, looking as if he wanted to interfere, but
not quite sure if it was a good idea.

Luther made up his mind for him when he pulled the Colt
from beneath his shirt. He pegged two shots into the floor in
front of his original two attackers, spraying their legs with wood
splinters. "You've got five seconds to be somewhere else," he
snapped.

Then he turned toward the bar and emptied the other four
rounds into the ranks of bottles behind the counter. The bartender
ducked down out of sight as broken glass and various liquids
sprayed all around him.

The room was suddenly empty. The remaining two attackers and the man by the table had run out the door. The bartender remained hidden somewhere below the bar. Only Snake-Eye was left, still howling and screaming, his eye riveted on his severed hand.

Luther thrust the pistol back into his waistband. Time for the final act. He walked out onto the boardwalk, headed over to his horse, and jerked the Winchester from its saddle scabbard. Sure enough, here he came, right on time, the sheriff, striding rapidly toward Luther. No deputy with him this time, Luther noticed, but the two men who'd been with Snake-Eye in the saloon were trailing along after the sheriff, a step or two behind, pointing at Luther, their mouths working overtime. "That's him!" one shouted, the man Luther had kicked in the groin. "He cut off Snake-Eye's arm!"

Luther stood, waiting, holding the rifle loosely. The sheriff stopped ten feet away, suddenly hesitant. "You're in big trouble, mister," he blustered. "Shootin' up my town. Usin' a knife on a man."

"No, Sheriff," Luther replied. "You're the one in trouble. But I suppose you don't recognize me."

The sheriff looked puzzled for a moment. Faint recognition was beginning to register in his eyes when Luther spoke again. "A man and a boy. Passing through. With a wagon and a good rifle. The same setup as today—almost. But this time I'm not letting go of my rifle."

The sheriff paled, stepped back a pace, his eyes locking onto the rifle. Which was pointed in the general direction of the ground. He might have completely backed down, but the man Luther had kicked in the groin, cursing loudly, suddenly pulled an old pistol out of his waistband. Maybe he figured he could make it, since he was half-hidden behind the sheriff, but Luther raised the rifle smoothly, almost to eye level, and shot the man through the right shoulder. The man spun around, his gun flying off to one side.

The sheriff, half-enveloped in a cloud of gun smoke, perhaps thinking he was the one who'd been fired at, clawed for his pistol. Luther had already jacked another round into the Winchester's firing chamber. By the time he got his shot off, the sheriff had his pistol up into firing position . . . just a yard away from the muzzle of the Winchester. Luther's bullet hit the sheriff in the hand, smashed against the metal of his pistol, then ricocheted off, pulverizing the bones in the sheriff's gun hand and wrist.

"That one was for me, Sheriff," Luther said. "The next one is for my father."

He levered another round into the chamber. The sheriff was half-hunched over, his left hand clamped over the bleeding mess that used to be his gun hand. Luther, barely aiming, shot the sheriff through the right knee. Screaming in agony, the sheriff went down, his leg folding at an unnatural angle.

Luther quickly worked the loading lever again. The sheriff was down, half out of his mind with the agony of his wounds. The man Luther had shot through the shoulder was sitting on the ground, looking as if he was going to faint. The only other man still in sight, one of those who'd tried to attack him in the saloon, was backing away quickly, his face white, his empty hands out in front of him. "I don't want no part of this, mister. I just wanna get the hell outta here!"

The man froze as the barrel of the Winchester tracked onto him. "The justice of the peace," Luther snapped. "Where is he?"

"He died, mister," the man babbled, hands still out and empty, his face white. "About six months ago. Drank hisself to death."

Luther nodded. Another form of justice had preceded him. He felt the adrenaline die down inside him. It was finished. The sheriff was lying on his side, his face bloodless from the pain of his ruined hand and knee. He would never use that gun hand again. And if he ever walked, it would be with a cane. The big man had passed out either from shock or loss of blood. From inside the saloon Snake-Eye's earlier screaming had sunk to low guttural moans.

Luther looked all around. He could see no one who might threaten him. He lowered the hammer on the Winchester, turned, and walked back to his horse. He mounted, but with the Winchester still in his right hand. He rode straight out of town, before anybody else decided to try their luck.

Another debt paid. But at a greater price this time. He'd shot a sheriff. A lawman. He'd put himself squarely on the other side of the law. That is, if anybody paid any attention to what had happened here. Everybody knew how corrupt the man had been, many would applaud his crippling. Still . . . a lawman. . . .

Luther was amazed by how calm he was. He punched a few more shells into the Winchester's loading gate. That was one of the things he liked most about it; you could load almost as you fired. A wonderful weapon.

He put the Winchester back into its scabbard, then began reloading the Colt. Never leave a weapon even partially empty. The Eleventh Commandment.

Luther made camp that night only several miles from Duncan Fife's mine. Where Fife had had his father murdered. It was tempting to ride on over to the mine, take on Fife and his hired thugs. Maybe kill Fife, or at least kill the men who'd actually murdered his father.

And probably die himself. Fife and the mine would be a hard nut to crack. The odds were way against Luther. He'd still do it some day . . . ride into that devastated valley, and go for Fife.

But not now. Not with unfinished business to settle. Logan and Stark. He'd go after them first. He'd keep his promise to Jedadiah. Logan and Stark, then Fife. Finally, one day, Duncan Fife would have to face justice. And in a land where official justice seldom touched the rich, it would have to be justice from the barrel of a gun.

Luther's gun.

CHAPTER
FOURTEEN

"Tom Logan? Sure, I know Tom Logan."

Luther fought back an urge to press the man harder. Instead, he merely grunted, as if what had just been said was not very important. "Is that so?" he asked casually. "Tell me . . . is he still running around with Jason Stark?"

"Well, hell yes, what else? Old Nick hisself an' his top devil, Beelzebub."

The man was talking too loudly. Luther took a quick look around the room. It was smoky, not too well lit, and there was a buzz of conversation, but the man's voice carried. Already, heads were turning in their direction. "Devil?" Luther asked absently.

The man laughed. Drunkenly. Luther had spent the past hour getting him this drunk. From the moment he'd walked into this grubby saloon, way out in the middle of nowhere, he'd sensed that it was a good hunting ground for information concerning the men he was after. The men he'd been tracking for so long.

Over two years. Of cold trails and wild-goose chases. At first it had appeared that Logan and Stark had vanished from the face of the earth. For a while Luther was terrified that someone else with a grudge had caught up with his quarry, and wiped them out.

From time to time he'd picked up little pieces of information, leading him this way and that. Once he'd come very close, missing them by only a couple of days. Then they'd vanished again. They'd probably taken a train. Luther was learning to hate trains. In just a few hours a train could take a person far away, without leaving any real trail.

The drunk was still talking. "Hell yes. Devils. They do rile people up. We're talkin' about a couple o' real catamounts, ol' Tom and Jase. Why, they been hittin' places all over this area."

"What do you mean?" Luther demanded, aware that his manner was growing just a little too sharp.

But the man was too drunk to notice. "Those boys got the best operation I ever seen. The only place they ever stay for more than a few days is way down in Mexico, where the law can't touch 'em. When they're short o' money, they just ride up over the border, hide out in the badlands, east o' here maybe a day's ride, make a hit, then head right back to Mexico."

"Have you ridden with them?" Luther asked.

"Well," the man said dismissively, "there was a time . . ."

"Johnson," a voice said from behind Luther, "you ain't never ridden much more'n a barroom chair. Or your mouth. You're talkin' too damned much."

Luther turned. A man was standing over him, just behind his chair. Like most of the men in the saloon, he had the look of a real hard case. Which was why Luther had started asking his questions. He'd heard rumors that Logan and Stark had become full-time outlaws. Many of the men here had that outlaw look about them. Like the man standing over him. They were Logan and Stark's kind of people.

"Just who the hell are you, mister?" the man asked, glaring at Luther. "You're askin' an awful lot of questions. What's your connection to Tom and Jason?"

Tom and Jason. First names. Luther turned away from the drunk, faced the newcomer. "I used to know both of 'em back around Colorado and Nebraska. We got separated. I been kinda wondering where they ended up."

The man's icy glare did not diminish. "Separated?" he asked drily. "You wouldn't be no lawman, would you, buddy? Maybe you tried to bring those boys in, once, and got . . . separated."

Luther replied, just as coldly. "Me and Tom and Jason, we shot up a town out in Nebraska a year or two ago. I got hit, couldn't travel for a while, lost track of 'em. As for lawmen, I use 'em for target practice."

Another long look. "So you say. All I know, mister, is that you ask more questions than you oughta. Now . . . what's your name?"

"Seems you like to ask questions, too," Luther replied coldly.

"That's right. And I'm still waitin' to hear your name."

Luther looked him straight in the eye. "Travis," he finally replied.

"Travis? Is that your first or last name?"

"That's the whole thing. Take it or leave it."

Other men were listening now. Some with interest, some with hostility. Luther was trying to figure how far he could push it. Too far, and the whole room might turn on him. And if he waffled, appeared weak, or confused, then they'd eat him alive.

The drunk suddenly broke in. "You know," he said, "this fella kinda reminds me of a wanted poster I saw a year or two back. About somebody who shot up a sheriff out Colorado way. The age'd be about right, but they didn't say nothin' about no moustache."

Luther's fingers strayed to the thick moustache he'd grown, brushed over it. The drunk laughed. "What happened, buddy? Grow the damn thing so's you'd look older?"

Luther said nothing, didn't even look at the drunk, kept his eyes fixed on the man standing by his chair.

"You the one that poster was talking about?" the man asked.

"Maybe," Luther said softly. "Maybe not."

Which was the right thing to say, what a wanted man was most likely to say in this kind of company. Neither denial nor agreement. Luther got to his feet. His face was only inches from the man who'd been questioning him. Luther looked him straight in the eyes, saw eyes as hard as his own. Neither man faltered. Luther stepped past the other man, then headed for the rear of the room. There was an outhouse out back. From time to time he'd noticed men heading in that direction.

He was aware of the man watching him. He was almost at the back door when he heard another man speak up. "Ya know, Hank, I remember somethin' Logan told me once. About some kid they shot up in Nebraska. Some kid who was on their trail, tried to bushwhack 'em."

"Well . . . I'll be a son of a bitch," Luther heard Hank say. "It could be. . . ."

Luther's hand was on the doorknob. "Hey, you!" Hank called out.

But Luther was already halfway through the door. Without looking back, he went outside. "Hey! Stop him!" he heard someone shout.

Luther stepped out into a narrow alleyway. He heard more shouting from behind, then the thud of boot heels against the saloon's wooden floor. Damn! His horse was tied up in front of the saloon, carrying all his gear, including his two rifles. He had nothing with him but his Colt and the knife.

But he was sure that if he'd headed for the front door, he'd never have made it at all. He began to run, heading away from the saloon toward a cluster of buildings. A shot sounded from behind him. A bullet churned up dirt six feet ahead.

Luther stopped behind the first of the buildings, pressing himself flat against one of its splintery sides. He drew the Colt. Two men were standing in the doorway he'd just left. One had a pistol in his hand and was trying to line up another shot. Luther fired first, two quick shots, not trying to hit either man, just sending lead into the door frame. Maybe if he didn't kill anybody they'd be a little less anxious to go after him.

The men, one cursing loudly, ducked back into the saloon. Luther turned and ran along the side of the building, keeping its bulk between him and the saloon. He could hear someone bellowing now, it sounded like Hank, "Get after him, boys! The idiot's goin' the wrong way!"

Yeah, the wrong way, Luther thought . . . if he continued to head in this direction. As usual, he'd made a wide circuit around the town before riding in, checking the layout. He knew that if he kept straight ahead he'd be pinned against a high cutbank at the far edge of town. But he immediately ducked to his left, still within the shelter of the buildings. Except for a couple of open places, he'd be sheltered all the way back to the main street.

He almost made it unseen, then a man stepped out in front of him. It was one of the men who'd been in the saloon. And he had a pistol in his hand.

Luther fired without thinking, while the man was still cocking his revolver. Luther's slug took the man in the chest. He flew backward, his pistol firing a bullet into the dirt. Then Luther was past him, not bothering to see how badly the man had been hit. He was tempted to run, but forced himself to slow to a walk, striding along as if he hadn't a care in the world.

He reached the main street. His horse was still at the hitching rack in front of the saloon, ears pricked up because of the firing. Luther walked straight to the mare, swung up into the saddle, and pulled her head around, ready to ride out of town.

But the men who'd been after him, alerted by the sound of the fight between Luther and the man he'd shot, were already pounding near; he could hear them panting and calling out to one another back in the alley.

Luther did not want a mob of men mounting up and chasing after him. Time to slow them down a little. The hell with trying to be nice.

He pulled his Winchester from its saddle scabbard and cranked back the hammer. Four men spilled out of the alley, guns in their hands, looking around wildly. By the time they spotted Luther, he was already riding straight at them, Winchester high. "Jesus!" one of them shouted, as horse and rider bore down on him.

Luther opened fire, eight shots, fast shooting, but well aimed. One man went down with a bullet in his head. Another spun to the side, clutching a shoulder. One turned and ran. Another tried to stand his ground, even got off a shot, which whizzed by Luther's left ear, but by then Luther was on him, the horse's weight spinning the man half around. Luther clubbed him over the head with the rifle barrel. The man fell.

Luther caught sight of more men in the alley. He paused for perhaps three seconds, sending another half dozen shots into the alley. It was a dangerous maneuver, because he was silhouetted out in the open, at the alley's mouth, but the man who'd run away, shouting in fear, chased by hot lead, had the effect of panicking the others. They all turned and ran, looking for better hiding places from which to shoot.

By then Luther was on the move again, spurring his mare out of town, and into the cover of some trees. Once out of sight, he immediately slowed his horse to a fast trot, then guided her onto a side trail that he knew would take him high above the other trails.

Half an hour later he reached a place where he could see way back down the trail. He stopped, sat his horse, and studied the landscape. He could see not only his back trail, but a great deal of the surrounding countryside. There was nobody in sight. If anyone was after him, they had taken a wrong turn.

Not that he'd really expected pursuit. He'd just shot it out with a bunch of hard cases, not the law. They'd remember, they'd try to cut him down if they ever ran across him again, but they were not likely to further risk their necks by chasing a man who'd already shown how hard he could bite.

Luther rode for another hour, until it began to grow dark. He made camp for the night, then lay in his bedroll for hours, looking up at the stars. He couldn't sleep; excitement was churning his

insides. He was close now, knew he was close, could taste it.
Logan and Stark. This was their area of operations . . . if he could
just track them down.

The Mexican border. That was a smart move, riding north to
rob, slipping back across the border into Old Mexico. United
States lawmen were not welcome below that border. But Luther
was no lawman. Quite the contrary. That drunk in the saloon had
a good memory. There actually had been a wanted poster out on
Luther . . . for crippling that crooked sheriff. The poster had more
or less dropped out of circulation, but he was still a wanted man.
He'd be in the Pinkerton files for sure.

Maybe he should just ride down into Mexico. Hunt for Logan
and Stark. But Mexico was a big place. He knew a little of the
lingo, but not a whole lot. He'd spent three months with a Mexican
girl; she'd taught him a little Spanish, although he didn't know
how much of her vocabulary he could use in polite company.

Maybe it would be better to head east, toward those badlands
the drunk had mentioned. If that was where Logan's bunch passed
through before and after a raid, maybe he could pick up their
trail again.

Such a long trail. It had been over two years since he'd ridden
away from Kathy's place. Two years of fruitless hunting. He'd
checked on Kathy once, discovered that she was indeed in San
Francisco, and drawing her money regularly. Banker Chase's
money. That had been one of the few positive achievements of
the past two years. That, and the Mexican girl. He smiled as
he remembered her. Maria was her name. For Luther, she had
completed an education Kathy had only started. But she had begun
to grow possessive, jealous, demanding, so Luther had simply
ridden away one day, richer in experience, and speaking a little
Mexican.

There had been other adventures. There was that time with the
Apaches. He'd figured he was going to lose his hair for sure, but
the Sharps had saved his bacon. Yes, some real adventures.

Lying in his bedroll, listening to the distant hooting of an
owl, Luther had to admit that the last two years had not been
all bad. He'd learned a lot. He'd matured. He never thought
of himself as a kid anymore. Nobody else seemed to, either.
Maybe it was the moustache. His hair was longer, too. He'd
started growing both, so that he'd be less easily recognized.
Now both had become part of his person. He liked the moustache, liked to run his fingers over it. Liked the feel of his

hair blowing around the back of his neck. Kept the sun off, too.

But, Logan and Stark. He'd ride north, start haunting those badlands and the area around. See if he could get a handle on Logan's bunch. Then follow them, wait for his chance. And maybe end this vendetta once and for all.

CHAPTER
FIFTEEN

The badlands were a maze of towering rock, twisted canyons, and sere volcanic flats. Genuine *mal país*, Luther thought. He knew that *mal país* meant bad land in Spanish.

Luther spent two weeks in this desolate area, mapping, in his mind, the terrain. If he did meet up with Logan and Stark, he wanted to know everything possible about his surroundings. He wanted every conceivable advantage.

The land was very dry. But there were springs. Over the past two years Luther had grown very good at finding water. Sometimes, from a high point, he would see a slight patch of green, which might mean a spring, or water just under the surface, easy to reach by digging. In this particular area there were quite a few springs. Some of them were near old Indian cliff dwellings.

These old ruins fascinated Luther. They were miniature cities, tucked away beneath huge overhangs, empty, spooky. Leaving his horse one day, he climbed up into a cliff dwelling, then wandered around the flat area in front of the buildings. He tried to imagine how the place must have been, maybe centuries ago—full of shouting, playing children, women grinding corn, men working on their weapons, or on sacred regalia. Human beings living not quite in total wilderness, but just at its edge, living as part of the earth, working with nature rather than against it, as was the case with Luther's own people. Standing in front of these old buildings, he could sense how their occupants must have felt, living with the idea of the world as something alive, something a human being could speak to, communicate with.

He did not stay overnight in any of the cliff dwellings; he would have had to leave his horse at the bottom of the cliff, way out of reach. He did find one old pueblo more or less at ground level, tucked away in the hollow of a low overhang. He could have put his horse in one of the half-ruined houses, but with the cliff at his back, he would have felt trapped.

Mostly, he camped near springs, close enough to have water available, but far enough away to miss the normal traffic that went to and from any water source in this dry land.

By the beginning of the third week, Luther felt that he knew the badlands fairly well. He also realized that, in its rough, broken vastness, he stood little chance of simply running across Logan and Stark and their gang.

There was a town not far away, a small, rough place pretty much like the seedy town where he'd so recently shot it out with those hard cases. He'd passed the town on his way into the badlands, and had noticed a telegraph line. It was connected, by that single line, to the outside world.

Luther decided to go to the town and monitor the telegraph. Maybe, when and if Logan's gang went into action, he'd hear about it over the wire.

Once in the town he kept out of sight as much as possible, except for trips to the telegraph office. He decided not to stay in the town's single grubby hotel, but took a room by the day, in a house owned by an elderly widow. Every day he went to the telegraph office and asked the clerk if he'd heard any interesting news. More days went by, days of inaction. Luther was beginning to wonder if the drunk in the saloon had been full of hot air about Logan's gang. Or maybe Logan and Stark were holed up permanently down in Old Mexico.

Boredom made Luther just the slightest bit careless. One day, walking back from the telegraph office, he was unaware of a man watching him. If Luther had seen the man, he might have recognized him as one of the hard cases who'd been in the saloon in that other town, where they'd come gunning for him. The man rode out an hour later, pressing his mount hard.

Luther's landlady saved his hide. She was a lonely old woman, her husband was long dead, and her sons had moved on. She pampered Luther, urged him to eat more of her starchy cooking than he really cared for, but he always treated her with great courtesy, as he figured any woman should be treated.

She came bursting into the house late one morning, puffing and out of breath, her pinched little face all flushed. Luther was immediately alert; something out of the ordinary must have happened. "There's some men just rode into town," she said, even before he could ask. "Real rough-looking men, an' they're asking about you. Everybody was acting dumb, but they're bound to find out. . . ."

Luther was already in motion. Most of his gear, except for his weapons, he kept in the stable behind the house. He reached into his pocket, pulled out a twenty dollar gold piece, and laid it on the kitchen table. "For what I owe you," he said.

"But you've already paid. . . ."

"Thanks, Mrs. Peters. I've enjoyed it here. I'll be back some-day."

He ran to his room and snatched up his rifles. He'd have to leave some of his clothing behind; there just wasn't time for packing. He ran back into the kitchen, and was headed out the back door when Mrs. Peters called after him, "They didn't strike me as bein' lawmen."

"They aren't."

He hurried into the barn, picked up his saddle, and threw it over his horse's back. The mare, sensing Luther's tension, played no tricks as he pulled the cinch tight. He hesitated about the bridle, but figured that the extra time it would take to put it on the horse might pay off later, if he had to ride hard. His rifles went into their saddle scabbards next, and only at the end did he load the horse down with his bedroll and saddlebags.

He'd taken too long; he could hear horses approaching. A lot of horses. He swung up into the saddle and pulled the mare's head toward the barn door. He slapped his heels hard against the horse's sides, while at the same time sliding the Winchester from its saddle scabbard. The mare gave a little jump of surprise, then bolted straight for the doorway.

As the horse ran out into the open, Luther had time only for general impressions . . . of a dozen or more horsemen riding at a fast trot toward the widow's house. Hard-looking men. They'd seen him now, several of them were looking in his direction. They were only about fifty yards away, and although it had been two years since he'd last seen them, Luther was sure he recognized two of the men. Tom Logan and Jason Stark.

"There he goes!" he heard someone shout; Luther thought it might have been Stark. Luther took the reins in his teeth, raised the Winchester, and opened fire, sending a fusillade of bullets toward the horsemen. He heard one man yelp, saw him grab at his arm, and then Luther was out of the yard, riding hell-for-leather in the opposite direction, heading toward the edge of town and the cover of a grove of cottonwood trees.

The shots he'd fired had caused considerable disorder among the horsemen; several had turned their mounts in various directions in an attempt to get out of the line of fire, and had collided. Men and horses were milling about wildly. One man fell from his saddle, simply by losing his balance. All of them were cursing and swearing. Before any of the men had drawn a gun, Luther was a hundred and fifty yards away.

They finally opened fire, a ragged volley. Luther heard lead whistling around him, but neither he nor his horse was hit. If they got his mare, that'd be the end. He'd be dead meat.

Luther reached the cottonwood grove well ahead of the men, who were now strung out in a ragged line, following him, whooping and hollering. Once inside the grove, Luther pulled his horse to a sliding stop behind a waist-high boulder, then jumped from the saddle. He spent several seconds cramming a few more rounds into the Winchester's loading gate, then he settled himself behind the rock, with the rifle's muzzle pointing down the trail. The men were now only about seventy yards away. Luther sighted carefully, not on a man, but on a horse.

He fired. The leading horse screamed, then went down hard, cartwheeling ass over teakettle. Its rider flew off to one side, and hit just as hard. Luther continued firing, aiming for horses, which were much easier targets. He hit two more before the riders, realizing that they were out in the open and easy targets, veered away to the sides, seeking shelter among the rocks and trees lining the trail.

Luther continued firing, although he knew he didn't have much chance of hitting anyone; all the men were out of sight by now. He did notice several riderless horses milling around, whinnying in fright. He shot two more of them before the remainder galloped away out of range.

Most of the men were on foot now, hidden behind cover. It would be a while before Logan, or Stark, or whoever was top honcho, got everything organized again. This was a good time, Luther figured, to get the hell out of here.

Leading his horse away, always keeping behind cover, he worked his way deeper into the grove. The men were shooting back now, bullets were slamming into trees and pinging off rocks, but none were coming very close to Luther and his horse. When he figured he was completely out of sight, he mounted, and rode out the back side of the grove.

It would not take Logan and Stark long to figure he was gone. Once they got their mounts sorted out, at least some of them would come after him. Or maybe they'd go back to town, to either buy or steal horses to replace the ones that had been shot. Either way, he'd probably get a big lead and have a chance to slip away from any pursuit.

He looked up at the sun. He figured it was an hour or so before noon. Darkness was a long ways off. If he could keep alive that long, he'd be able to use the darkness.

He'd been riding for an hour before he noticed any pursuit. Cresting a hill, he saw, over a mile back, three horsemen, coming on hard. They'd played it smart, sending some of the men after him, while the others got new mounts. Luther rode down the back side of the hill, wondering if they'd spotted him while he was at its crest. If so, they'd probably increase their pace.

Well, he'd made contact with Logan and Stark all right, if not exactly in the manner he'd hoped for. Word must have spread about the fight at the saloon, about someone looking for Tom Logan and Jason Stark. Someone else had obviously spotted him in town, it didn't matter who. The fat was in the fire.

The trail Luther had been following headed into the badlands. He forced himself to recollect what lay ahead. There were some broken canyons, then a long open slope, leading up to an escarpment. If he could just make that escarpment before the others caught up to him. . . .

It was very hot by the time Luther reached the bottom of the escarpment; the sun was a couple of hours past its zenith. A steep trail led, through a water canyon, up to the top of an otherwise sheer cliff. Luther looked down at his horse. The mare was beginning to blow a little; she'd been pushed hard. Luther leaned forward, putting his mouth a few inches from the horse's ears. "Come on, old girl," he said softly, as he set the mare at the steep trail. "Just a little further, and then you can rest."

Halfway up the trail, Luther looked back. The riders were closer now, maybe half a mile away. And there were now five of them, rather than three. Two more had caught up. Luther urged a little more speed out of his horse. The mare was heaving by the time they reached the top. Luther rode the horse away from the edge of the escarpment, then dismounted. He quickly untied his bedroll, and tossed it closer to the edge of the cliff. He reached for a rifle,

the Sharps this time. Taking his cartridge pouch, he walked over
toward the cliff and his bedroll.

He lay prone. The tightly rolled bedding made a fine rest for
the Sharps. Luther looked out over the flats below. The riders
were much closer now, perhaps only five hundred yards away.
He wished that he could study them through his binoculars, to see
if Logan and Stark were among them. But he didn't have time;
they were too damned close.

He raised the rifle's rear sight, then reached forward to slide the
crossbar up to the four-hundred-yard position. He cranked back
the hammer, set the trigger, then settled down to aim.

The riders were coming straight at him; he would not have to
allow for windage. He sighted on the first man, relaxing totally,
stilling his breathing. When he had the man in his sights, he held
his breath, his body draped loosely over the rifle, his finger
exerting steady pressure against the trigger.

The rifle seemed to go off by itself. The butt slammed back
against Luther's shoulder. A big cloud of acrid white smoke shot
out of the barrel, then drifted away on a light breeze.

The huge bullet, coming from above, hit the man Luther had
been aiming at square in the chest, smashing him back over the
haunches of his horse. He was dead before he hit the ground.
By then Luther was already reloading, pulling the big hammer
back to half cock, flipping open the breach, cramming another
paper cartridge into the chamber, then slamming the chamber
shut. It took another second and a half to press a copper cap
onto the nipple, pull the hammer back to full cock, and begin
aiming again.

The men, surprised by the shot, had stopped in place . . . which
made Luther's second shot all the easier. Another man was hit,
this time in the shoulder. His arm was ripped half off his body.
He lay on the ground, stunned, only semi-conscious, great gouts
of blood pumping from the terrible wound.

The men below had seen the second big puff of gun smoke from
the top of the escarpment. Logan was one of them. After a quick
glance around, he shouted to the remaining two men, "We're out
in the open, boys. We gotta get to cover."

They split up, riding off in opposite directions. Luther fired
again, but the men were already in motion, and he missed. By the
time he had reloaded, the three men had gained a hundred yards.
He fired a fourth time, hitting a horse. The animal went down,
screaming. Luther saw the rider roll clear, hesitate for a moment,

draw his pistol, then shoot the animal through the head.

Luther was furiously reloading. He wished he'd taken the trouble to have the Sharps converted to cartridges; he'd be able to fire much more quickly. By the time he had another cartridge in the chamber, all of the men were out of sight, either behind rocks, or hidden in little arroyos.

The men below began to fire back, but since they only had saddle guns, either Winchesters or Henrys, their shots fell short of Luther's hiding place. He fired from time to time, whenever he saw movement, but the distance was considerable, and the targets small. Because of the Sharps's great accuracy he was able to force the men to keep their heads down. Nobody would be coming for him until after dark.

It was about two hours before sundown when Luther noticed a cloud of dust from way back down the trail. In a little while horsemen came into sight. By now, Luther had fetched his binoculars. He studied the horsemen. There were eight of them, plus some extra mounts. They must have cleaned the widow's town of horseflesh, probably just stole them. Luther thought he recognized one of the men as Jason Stark. Which meant that Tom Logan must be one of those who'd originally followed him. So, they were both down there . . . unless Logan was one of the men he'd shot.

Luther settled into place, waiting for the riders to come nearer. He had no intention of aiming at Stark; he'd prefer to be face-to-face when he put a bullet into Jedadiah's killers. He'd want to look into their eyes.

But the men already hidden below shouted a warning to the approaching horsemen. Luther fired as they raced toward cover, but he only managed to hit another horse. By the time he had reloaded, all of the men were under cover.

Luther soon discovered that a new element had been added to the game. One of the newcomers had a big-bore rifle, a Sharps, or maybe a Ballard. Luther saw a big puff of smoke from behind a rock, and a moment later a heavy bullet gouged out a big chunk of cliff only a foot or two from his head.

With his face stinging from particles of dirt that had been driven against his skin, Luther immediately scooted backward. Then he approached the edge of the cliff five yards further along, and peered over cautiously, showing only one eye.

Nothing. Not a person moving. He studied the rock from which the smoke had come. He thought he saw a slight movement, but could not be certain.

Running back to his horse, which was far enough from the
precipice to be out of sight, Luther pulled an old shirt out of
his saddlebags. Picking up a stick, he ran back to the edge of
the cliff; he hated leaving the men below out of his sight.

He put the shirt on the end of the stick, then propped stick and
shirt against a bush, so that both would be visible from below. He
rolled to the side, the Sharps ready.

Once again there was a big puff of smoke from behind the
rock. The shirt Luther had propped up went flying backward.
Luther aimed at the little bit of movement he could see behind
the rock, and cranked off a round. After the roar of the shot had
faded away, he heard a cry from below. He was pretty sure it had
come from the rock, or near it. He'd either scared the hell out of
someone, or hit him hard.

A few minutes later another shot came from below. The bullet
passed harmlessly overhead; since Luther was staying out of sight,
the rifleman had nothing to aim at.

Over the next half hour, Luther fired two more shots, each time
rolling out of the way as soon as he'd fired. Both times there was
an answering shot. Uncomfortably close. Someone down there
could sure as hell shoot.

Luther left a stick propped up near the edge of the cliff. He
hoped that from below it would look like the barrel of a rifle.
Keeping low, he moved back to his horse. He shoved the Sharps
back into its saddle scabbard, and fastened his bedroll back in
place. He led the mare away about fifty yards before mounting;
he did not want anything to show above the cliff edge.

Riding away, Luther reviewed what he knew of the terrain
ahead. The back side of the escarpment descended gradually
to an area of deep gullies. Beyond the gullies there was more
broken country, choked by thick brush . . . an area in which a
hunted man would be able to hide himself easily. The kind of
land where Luther would be able to strike back at the men chasing
him. He was about to change from hunted to hunter.

CHAPTER SIXTEEN

Luther made no attempt to hide his trail. He wanted to make certain he was followed . . . up to a point.

He rode until an hour after dark, then branched off to his right, finally stopping in a little depression next to a narrow pass, where the trail ran between sheer cliffs. If by some chance, or skill, his pursuers were able to follow him this far, he should be able to hold them off long enough to slip away through the pass.

He catnapped during the night, finally rising an hour before dawn. Saddling his mare, he rode on through the pass, once again leaving a clear trail. Unless Logan, Stark, and company had no trailing ability at all, they'd follow him easily enough.

About ten in the morning he reached the area he'd been looking for. Over the past few miles the terrain had been flat, with light brush cover, not enough to impede his progress, but enough so that it was difficult to see more than twenty or thirty yards ahead. He rode carefully now, remembering what lay ahead. He reached the place he was looking for a few minutes later, stopping his horse at the edge of a sheer drop-off.

It was as he'd remembered. In the middle of flat, level ground, some ancient catastrophe had made a deep chasm in the earth, at least fifty feet deep. And very narrow—the far side was only about twenty feet away. Light brush grew right up to the edge. The chasm was so well-concealed that the first time Luther had been by this way he'd nearly ridden his horse right into it.

He turned toward his right, riding along the edge of the chasm into much thicker brush. He now took great pains to conceal where he had turned. Dismounting, he took off his boots and put

118

on his moccasins, so that he would leave no heel prints. He cut a
length of brush that had feathery foliage at its end, and began to
sweep away his tracks, to the point where they disappeared into
the thicker brush. Now, all that a pursuer would see, unless he
was a very good tracker, were the hoofprints of Luther's horse,
leading right up to the edge of the chasm.

Luther rode for more than two miles along the edge of the
chasm, until it began to grow more shallow. A mile further along
it ended in a small depression, which Luther easily crossed. Then
he turned to his left and rode along the far side of the chasm,
pushing his horse a little now, because he suspected he did not
have much time. He had no doubt that Logan's bunch was still on
his trail. The only question was, how fast were they moving?

Half an hour later he reached a point along the edge of the
chasm directly across from where his tracks ended on the other
side. He stopped his horse in heavy brush about fifty yards back
from the edge. Tying the reins to a thick bush, he sat down
to wait.

Half an hour passed. Forty-five minutes. Then he thought he
heard a horse snort, perhaps two hundred yards away. He saw his
mare's ears prick up. Standing, Luther clamped a hand over the
animal's nostrils to keep her from snorting back.

He began to see flickers of movement through the brush on the
far side of the chasm. Luther untied his horse's reins, then began
to lead the animal closer to the edge, always keeping within the
thickest cover.

More movement from the other side, more sound: the voices
of men, mixed with the jingle of bridles and spurs, and the creak
of saddle leather. A muffled oath. He saw them, then, ride out of
the brush about forty yards from the far side of the chasm. Luther
mounted, still hidden behind thick brush, hoping they would not
see the crown of his hat. He was now only about thirty yards from
the chasm's edge on his own side. But here, the brush was thicker.
On the far side the only thick brush was right near the edge of the
drop-off. Hiding it, he hoped, from Logan's bunch.

It was Logan and Stark, all right, and what Luther had left alive
of their crew. Hard to count them in the brush, maybe nine or ten
men, riding close together. As they picked their way through the
brush, their eyes appeared to be focused mostly on the ground.
Only a couple of men were looking straight ahead.

It was these men who first saw Luther as he rode out of the
brush, Winchester in hand, and charged straight at them. The

rifle went to his shoulder, and he began firing. The range was about fifty yards; both he and the others were quite near the chasm.

Consternation among Logan's men, some of whom were clawing for weapons, others trying to jerk their horses around. Luther veered, cutting across in front of them, firing fast. He saw one man fall, apparently hit hard. Another twisted in the saddle, clutching at his ribs.

Then Luther was gone, arcing away through thick brush, disappearing behind some large boulders. He heard curses and shouts from the men behind him, then a bellow from Logan, "Don't just sit there on your nags, you lunkheads! Git the hell after the son of a bitch!"

The whinny of horses, a rush of hooves, then one man cried out, apparently someone who knew the area well, "Hey! Wait! Don't ride . . ."

Luther had stopped his horse behind the boulders. He peered over the top. Three or four men were already strung out in a line, pounding toward him. Then they reached the light brush at the edge of the chasm. The man in front saw the drop-off more quickly than the ones behind, and tried to rein his horse in, but the others were right on his tail. There was a collision, and the leading horse and rider disappeared over the edge of the chasm. Luther heard a wild human shout, mingled with the terrified scream of a horse, and then a crash, as both man and horse hit the jagged rocks piled at the bottom of the chasm.

The other riders had pulled up sharply. "Goddamn!" one of them shouted. Others were riding closer. For just a few seconds all eyes stared down into the chasm. "Sam!" one man called downward. "Are you all right?"

"Looks like he broke his fool neck," another replied.

Luther slid the Sharps from its scabbard, cranked back the hammer, holding the trigger back until the rifle was at full cock, so that there would be no noise. He sighted for a second. At this range, it was such an easy shot.

"Watch what you're doin'. The bastard is still out there somewhere," one man snarled to the others . . . a moment before Luther blew the head off one of the riders. There was another mad scramble away from the edge of the chasm, back into the brush. Luther rammed the Sharps back into its scabbard and jerked out the Winchester, but it was too late. Men were scattering into the brush; the three shots he fired all missed.

It was time to leave. The men were shooting back. A couple of bullets pinged off the rock in front of Luther, scattering chips. Other bullets flew wide. Luther turned his horse's head and rode away, doing his best to keep the boulders between himself and Logan's crew. He did not have to fear them coming after him; the chasm was too wide to jump a horse across.

Within seconds he was hidden by thick brush. He nudged the mare into a trot. Time to make tracks. And leave plenty of them behind. Once again, Luther made no attempt to hide his trail. Let them follow him . . . once they found a way around that big gash in the ground. For Luther, the game had only begun. Before he finished he'd make Tom Logan and Jason Stark, and every man jack riding with them, wish they'd never heard of Jedadiah Bass.

It was a long, tiring day. Luther had no choice but to keep riding, trying to put distance between himself and the men following. On two occasions he rode across areas sheeted in rock, where he would not leave a trail. Both times he turned off in another direction before reaching the far side. It would take his pursuers a while to pick up his trail again.

But they came on faster than he'd expected. Cresting a rise, he saw them about a mile back, strung out along the trail. They'd learned not to bunch up. He took out his binoculars. Nine men, one riding hunched over in the saddle. Probably the one who'd clutched his side back at the chasm. Luther wondered how badly he was hit. Not so badly that he couldn't ride.

Luther took out the Sharps again, steadied it on a rock. He waited until the column was about half a mile away. A long shot. He set the crossbar on the rear sight very high, then studied the landscape for signs of wind. A gentle breeze was coming from his right. He doubted there was much breeze at all below; he would not have to compensate very much

He took a long time aiming, waited until the men were strung out along the trail in a line stretching straight away from him. The Sharps roared, smoke billowed. Luther laid down the rifle and stood watching. It took a long time for the bullet to reach the men. He'd been aiming at the front man. A horse suddenly fell, further back along the column. He'd overshot, but since they were all lined up, he'd managed to hit something. Damned lucky shot.

Luther quickly reloaded. The men were scattering off the trail as he fired again. No one, man or horse, appeared to be hit, but Luther knew he'd shaken them.

He picked up his binoculars and scanned the area. Most of the men had taken cover. He could make out a couple of horses, half-concealed behind brush. He was tempted to try to hit more horses; the men must be about out of spare mounts by now. If he could force some of them to ride double, that'd slow them even more.

He decided to ride on before the man with the big-bore rifle got a bead on him. They'd all go to ground for a while, wondering where the hell he'd pop up next. When no more shots came, they'd continue on after him. But probably with much more caution.

A wall of brush lay ahead. Luther rode into it. The brush was so thick that it was difficult to see more than a few yards in any direction. The land was broken and rough.

Luther now began to carefully conceal his trail. Logan's bunch should have little trouble following him right up to where the brush began. After that, he hoped they'd completely lose him. If they did not find him by dark, he'd have the edge.

He heard them when they rode into the brushy area an hour later, heard their muttered curses as thorns caught at their clothing. But they were much more quiet now, much more subdued. Perhaps they were beginning to realize that they were as much hunted as hunters.

Luther had ridden around in a big arc. He was now behind Logan's bunch. He shadowed along after them, keeping about a quarter of a mile away, following their tracks easily. When it began to grow dark, he stopped, figuring they'd do the same. Half an hour later he saw the glow of a camp fire, its light clearly penetrating the brush. Careless of them. Very careless.

Luther let another hour pass. He tied his horse to a bush in a grassy depression, where it would be able to graze. Wearing his moccasins again, and carrying the Winchester, he ghosted silently through the brush. It took him a long time to cover the four hundred yards to the fire. He could see it more clearly now, a good-sized fire. Old Jedadiah had told him many times that white men tended to build far too big a camp fire. "Those Injuns knew how to make a sensible fire," Jedadiah had said. "Remember, always keep it small, just a few dry sticks, enough to boil water, or heat some jerky, but not big enough to be seen more than a few yards away. Keep yer fire hidden . . . and you'll keep yer hair."

Luther stopped about forty yards from the campsite. It was very dark; there was no moon, the only light was from the

stars, and from the camp fire . . . which effectively blinded the
men grouped near it. They would see nothing but a blank wall
of night all around them.

The men were sprawled around the fire, some eating, some
lying on bedrolls. The features of most were lost in shadow, but
he could make out Stark, sitting by the fire, flipping a pocketknife
at a patch of grass. Luther heard a man groan. He saw Stark turn
toward somebody lying on a bedroll. Another man got up from
the fire, walked over to the man on the bedroll. "You doin' okay,
Milt?" he asked.

"Hurts," the man lying down said. "You gotta get that bullet
outta me."

Another voice cut in. Luther thought it was Logan's. "You'll
get it out when we reach someplace where we can chase down
a sawbones. Unless you want it butchered out right here, with no
water around for miles. . . ."

"We should head for a town first thing in the morning," the
other man said, the one who'd gone over to talk to the wounded man.

It was Stark who answered. "No. We're gonna keep on that
bastard's trail till we run him to ground. If we don't kill him now,
he'll just keep comin' at us."

"Jesus," the other man burst out. "He's already killed four of
us, put a pill in Milt's side, and winged Henry. I think we oughta
just get the hell outta here."

"You ain't here to think, Jeff."

It was Logan's voice again. Luther could just barely make out
a form further from the fire, half-hidden under a shelf of brush.
"We go after him till he's dead," Logan snapped. "Then we ride
on home."

The man named Jeff grumbled a little, but Luther could tell that
he did not care to tangle horns with Logan, not alone, and none
of the other men were backing him. "I want his ass, too," one of
them said. "No son of a bitch shoots a horse out from under me
and lives to tell about it."

There was a little more muttering, some in agreement, then the
camp began to settle down. They must be tired, as Luther was
tired. He watched as Stark set a night guard. It was well thought
out; Luther wondered if Stark had military experience. Two men
were posted with the horses, right at the edge of camp, with an
impenetrable wall of brush behind them. There was no way for
Luther to get to the horses. Too bad. He'd considered running off

the gang's mounts, then hunting the men down in the brush, one by one.

There was also a walking perimeter guard. "You stay in the brush," Stark warned him. "Just outside the firelight. Walk for a while, then stop and listen. If anything moves, anything at all, blast it. We ain't got no friends around these parts."

The camp settled down. Soon, all but the guards appeared to be asleep. One man cursed at another who was snoring loudly. The snoring subsided for a while, then resumed again. Good. The snores would cover any sounds Luther might make.

Midnight approached. Luther had spent a long time studying the perimeter guard's movements. The man was doing as Stark had ordered; making a slow circuit of the camp, with frequent stops to look and listen. Most of the stops lasted for at least five minutes.

Deciding that now was the time, with the men asleep and the guards growing tired, Luther waited until the perimeter guard was over by the men watching the horses, then he took position at a point where he'd already seen the guard pause several times. The point in his rounds that was furthest from the camp.

Luther stood hidden in a thick clump of brush. His rifle lay within easy reach, but his knife was in his hand, ready. It felt good against his palm, balanced, deadly. He remained motionless for fifteen minutes, then he heard, rather than saw, the guard approaching. Luther tensed, waiting for him to come within range.

But he did not. He stopped several feet short of where Luther was hidden. Standing in one spot, the guard turned in a full circle, scanning the area around him. Luther froze, hiding the knife beneath his arm, afraid that the blade might gleam in the starlight, and give him away. For several seconds the guard seemed to be looking straight at him. Luther flexed his knees a little, ready to go for his pistol before the guard could bring up his rifle.

But the guard turned away again, walked up to some brush, poked at it with the barrel of his rifle, then started on his rounds again.

His route took him right by where Luther was hidden. Bored, certain that there was no one around, the man was walking unconcernedly. Luther's left hand came snaking around from behind, clamping over his mouth, jerking his head back. One wide slash from the huge knife, and the man's throat was cut nearly to the vertebrae. He thrashed for a moment, clawing at Luther's hand, his rifle falling noisily to the ground, then he suddenly collapsed, his brain starved of blood.

The falling rifle had made way too much noise. "What the hell's goin' on over there, Pete?" a voice called out from the direction of the horse herd. Luther bent, picked up his own rifle, and pulled back the hammer. The fire had died down to glowing coals, but Luther could vaguely make out the shapes of men, some sitting up in their bedrolls, one man actually on his feet.

Luther opened fire, six fast shots, aiming at the man who was standing. He knew he hit him at least once, because the man went flying backward, shouting in pain.

Then Luther was gone, jinking to one side, running back into the brush in the direction from which he'd come. Guns were going off all over the camp now, sending lead into the brush. Not a single shot came near Luther.

He crouched about fifty yards from the camp. Some of the men were still yelling. Then someone snarled a command, and they quieted down. There was some muttering, then Luther heard a man say, "Taylor's dead. Shot right through the middle. Twice." ·

"Where is that goddamn guard?" Stark snarled.

There was a rustling of movement, then a couple of minutes later someone called out, his voice disgusted, "Got his throat cut. Ear to ear."

Now Luther could hear the man Logan had called Jeff speaking again. "I told you!" he cried. "We gotta get outta here. Before that wild man kills us all!"

Luther heard a sharp smacking sound, followed by a yelp of pain. Then Logan's voice. "And I told you . . . we go after the bastard until we get him. His horse has gotta be worn-out. We'll run him down tomorrow. Now, some of you boys get out in that brush. See if you can find the son of a bitch."

More muttering. "Not me," one voice said loudly enough for Luther to hear. "Not in the dark."

Luther smiled. He doubted that either Logan or Stark had enough control over the men to get them to wander through thick brush in the middle of the night, with the prospect of being ambushed by the man who'd cut the perimeter guard's throat. Most white men were squeamish about knives . . . which was why Luther had used his. He didn't dare approach the camp again, but he doubted that any of the men would get much sleep tonight.

An argument began. Oddly, it was Stark arguing with Logan. "I say we cut our losses, get the hell back down over the border,"

Stark insisted. "Try for the bastard another time."

"He'll just keep comin' at us," Logan argued back. But his voice was beginning to lack conviction. From his hiding place in the brush, Luther listened as Stark wore Logan down. Most of the men seemed to be behind Stark. After all, they were the ones doing all the dying, chasing a man who they realized wanted only Logan and Stark.

Finally, Luther heard a curse from Logan, then an object hitting the ground, as if he'd thrown something down in disgust. "Okay," he snarled. "We head south first thing in the morning. Meanwhile, we keep one hell of a sharp lookout. Throw lead if you hear any sound at all."

Luther did not know if he liked what he'd just heard. The gang would be heading for Mexico. If he tried to ride in after them, he'd stand out like a sore thumb.

But what choice did he have? Wherever they headed, he would follow. All the way to hell . . . if that's what it took.

Luther moved silently back to his horse, untied the animal, and rode what he considered a safe distance. He needed sleep, rest, but he was worried that they might find him while he was asleep. He chose a place half a mile from the main trail, unsaddled his horse, put a hackamore in her mouth, stuffed a little beef jerky in his own mouth, then stretched out on the ground without even laying out his bedroll. He was asleep before he'd completely chewed the jerky.

He was awakened by the sun shining in his eyes. He sat up, blinking, cursing himself for having slept too long. He immediately slapped all his gear onto his horse, and was ready to ride in a few minutes. No time for breakfast. Chewing more jerky, he headed for the highest ground in the area. When he reached it, he dismounted, and began studying the terrain through his binoculars.

Nothing in sight. There was only one main trail leading south. Had Logan and Stark's bunch taken some other route? Would he be able to find their tracks? Or maybe they hadn't left at all. Maybe they were holed up somewhere nearby, waiting for him. If he went looking for a trail, he'd have to ride back into the brush, where he would be just as susceptible to ambush as they were.

He swept the binoculars further to his left, halted, swept back. He'd caught a glimpse of movement, perhaps a mile away. He steadied the binoculars. Yes. A file of men, it looked like half a dozen, maybe seven. About what Logan's band had shrunk down to.

Luther mounted and set off in pursuit. A distant pursuit. He wanted to hang back far enough so that, even if they saw him, he would not be worth chasing. He spotted them two more times later that day, a couple of miles distant, still heading south at about the same pace. Either they had not seen him, or did not care, just as long as he stayed well away.

Luther spent most of the day trying to figure out his next move. They were wary now; he doubted he'd be able to surprise them again. At least not before they reached Mexico. And once in Mexico, what then? He had no idea what kind of setup they might have down there, how many he'd have to face. And it'd be on their own ground.

He had to get around in front of them again, set up another ambush, even if it was risky. If he could whittle their numbers down far enough, the best thing to do might be to just have it out with two or three survivors, face-to-face. He decided he'd continue riding after they made camp, look for a good place to surprise them tomorrow.

Half an hour later he noticed a large number of vultures circling, about a mile ahead, off to one side of the trail. He rode more cautiously now, studying the tracks the others had left. As far as he could make out, the tracks had been made by seven horses. That should be about right; most of their spare horses were dead, or had run off during the fighting.

As he approached the area where the vultures were circling, he hesitated. There were fewer vultures now; either some had left, or they had landed. He caught sight of movement about a hundred yards from the trail, something black, a seething mass of black. It must be the vultures, feeding on something. He studied them through his binoculars. Damn . . . it looked like they were feeding on a human body!

Luther's first impulse was to ride over and take a look. But he feared a trap. So, instead of riding off to the side, he continued along the trail for another half-mile. There were the same number of tracks, the same seven horses. He was about to turn around and head for the vultures when he noticed something curious about the tracks . . . some of the horses seemed to be walking awfully light. And they kept straying off to the side. As if they were being led.

Luther immediately rode off the trail. He took out his binoculars and studied a hill, far ahead. Sure enough, he spotted a file of horsemen climbing the hill. He counted slowly. It looked like six men and a led horse. Shouldn't there be seven men? But then, there was the body he thought he'd seen beneath that mass of vultures. Could it be the man he'd hit in the side? Perhaps he'd died along the trail, and they'd simply left him for varmints to eat.

He was about to turn and head back toward the vultures, but he took another moment to study the riders. They were very far away, but there seemed to be something odd about the way two or three of them were riding. They did not look right. Dummies? Tied onto horses?

Now he did head back for the vultures, but in a big circle, so that when he rode in, he came at them from behind the trail. He stopped his horse in a patch of brush, and sat for five minutes, studying the landscape.

The number of vultures had grown, an obscene black mass writhing and struggling above what definitely did look like a human body. No faking the vultures' enthusiasm. He was probably being foolish, too careful. He should just ride over there, run the vultures off, and see if the body was the man he'd shot in the side.

Then he noticed, about forty yards from the body, a flock of quail suddenly break cover and rush away, skimming just above the ground on their short wings. He also noticed that the vultures on that side of the body were nervous, edging away from a particular patch of brush.

Out came the binoculars again. At first Luther saw nothing. Then, finally able to pick individual details out of a mass of foliage and shadows, he saw an object too perfectly straight to be natural. And at one end of that object, something else, something moving in an unnatural manner. Too big a movement to blame on the faint breeze that was sweeping over the area.

The objects now became clear to Luther. A rifle barrel, with a hat above the stock. Damn if they hadn't set a trap for him! They'd put dummies on some of the horses, all right, and left a welcoming committee, hoping he'd go investigate the vultures.

A few more minutes study, and Luther made out two other men, hidden within a few yards of the first. Despite a careful study of nearby areas, he could see no one else. Foolish of them to group all the members of an ambush party together. They should have spread out. Hell, maybe they had spread out. Maybe there were others hidden whom he simply could not see.

Not likely. They no longer had enough men for such an elaborate ambush. He'd bet on there only being three of them. He'd bet on it with his life.

He rode around in another circle, so that he would be coming at the men from behind. He finally reached a place where he could see all three of them, sprawled out on the ground behind some bushes, facing the vultures and the body, waiting for their nemesis's curiosity to lead him into their trap.

He'd have to make his move before they spotted him. Slipping his Winchester from its scabbard, he took the reins in his mouth, kicked his horse in the ribs, and charged.

He was only about sixty yards away from the three men when they became aware of the pounding of hooves from behind them. They twisted around, one more slowly than the others, and, to their amazement, saw a lone horseman racing straight at them.

Using his heels to zigzag his mount from side to side, Luther opened fire. One man already had his rifle to his shoulder, but he was still turning when he fired. He overtracked the barrel . . . and missed. He had no second chance to shoot; Luther's bullet took him right in the center of the chest, knocking him over backward.

The second and third man each got off two shots. Luther felt one bullet tear through his shirt, burning the skin under his arm. Another bullet knocked his hat from his head, but his own bullets were finding their marks. "I'm hit, Jason!" one of the men yelled.

By then Luther had raced by them, disappearing behind a wall of brush. He instantly slid from the saddle, letting his horse go on past. The animal continued to run for another hundred yards, then stopped, prancing in a nervous circle.

The man who'd been hit had called out to someone named Jason. Jason Stark? Luther hoped so. Running around to the side, he approached the ambush spot from a new direction. His rifle was up and ready, cocked. He was panting a little, which might throw off his aim, but he wanted to get back to the men before they recovered from his first attack.

He came at them from his own right, their left. He immediately saw that the man he'd shot first was lying just as he'd last seen him. Probably dead. Another man was holding his side, his rifle trailing from his right hand. And the third man was indeed Jason Stark.

Stark had seen Luther, and was bringing up his rifle. Luther and Stark fired almost at the same instant, but Luther had a moment

more to aim. His bullet hit Stark low in the abdomen, driving
the air from his body. Stark staggered backward. His own shot
had missed. But now the other man had seen Luther. He raised
his rifle, clumsily because of his wound. Luther was closer now,
only thirty yards away. He shot the man through the head.

A bullet burned across Luther's cheek. He immediately rolled
to one side, seeking shelter behind some brush. He caught a
glimpse of Stark, hunched over with pain, but still deadly, rifle
in hand.

Luther let his roll carry him right on through the brush and back
onto his feet. He came up shooting. His first shot took Stark in the
left leg. Stark dropped down on one knee. But he was still not out
of action, he was still dangerous. He raised his rifle and got off
another shot. A wild shot. Luther watched as Stark struggled with
the loading lever on his Winchester. He was weakening fast.

Luther walked straight at Stark, working the loading lever
methodically as he put three more bullets into his enemy. "This
is for Jedadiah," he called out, surprised by how calm he sounded,
because inside, he was burning with anger, remembering how
Jedadiah had died.

Even with so much lead in him, Stark was still up on one knee.
But he was no longer firing. The muzzle of his rifle now rested
on the ground. Luther watched as Stark tried to raise the rifle, tried
to get off one more shot. Inch by inch the muzzle rose. "You crazy
son of a . . ." Stark snarled.

Luther put a final bullet into the center of Stark's chest. The
impact drove Stark over onto his back, with one leg doubled
beneath him. The rifle fell clear. Luther walked up close, levering
another round into the chamber.

There was no need for any mare shooting. Stark's eyes were
half open, staring sightlessly up at the sky. His legs twitched a
few times, then he lay completely still.

Looking down at Stark, Luther nodded slowly. "It's almost
over, Jedadiah," he murmured. "Two down . . . and one to go."

CHAPTER SEVENTEEN

Luther did not know how long he stood over Stark's body. He came to himself with a start. What the hell was he doing standing here? Logan and the others, having heard the shooting, would undoubtedly be on their way back with the horses, to pick up Stark and the two men with him. They'd get a surprise.

Luther started toward where he'd left his horse. On the way, he passed the vultures; they were still swarming all over the body. He put a couple of bullets into the ground near the corpse. The vultures scattered, some managing to take off, others too bloated with the body's flesh to fly. They hopped along in an obscene manner, their huge wings trailing the ground.

Luther walked closer to the body. It was a man, all right, wearing trail clothes. Or had been a man. There wasn't much left of the face. He could only assume that it was the man he'd wounded in the side the day before. He must have died along the trail. They'd used him to bait a trap . . . which had slammed shut on Stark, rather than Luther.

Luther's horse was standing forty yards away, cropping grass. Luther walked up to the animal, which moved away a few steps. He immediately noticed that the horse was limping. "Take it easy . . . take it easy," he said softly. Catching the bridle, he bent and lifted one of the animal's forelegs. Damn. The shoe was coming loose. Logan and the others were undoubtedly on their way, and he had a lame horse.

Luther led the mare toward a patch of thick brush. He had to find cover. The mare limped along after him. Luther wondered if she could run at all. Not likely, with that shoe partially dangling.

Maybe, if he found good enough cover, he could work on the shoe, drive the nails back into the hoof. But that would make noise, and possibly alert Logan and company.

He led the horse deeper and deeper into the thicket. He was trying to figure how many men Logan had left. Two? Three? He considered taking them on, finishing the job now. But, with his horse lame, it would be close to suicide.

He heard them when they rode up, the muffled chunking of their horses' hooves against the soft sandy soil near where Stark and the others lay dead. He was about two hundred yards away when the bodies were discovered, but he was able to hear, faintly, Logan's violent swearing.

Luther reached into his saddlebags and pulled out a box of Winchester ammunition. He immediately began shoving rounds into the rifle's loading gate. Stuffing his pockets with more shells, he headed back the way he had just come, on foot, leaving his horse hidden in the thicket.

When he was about eighty yards away, he was able to overhear most of the conversation between Logan and his men. "Jesus," one man was saying. "He's killed nine of us so far. And I figure he ain't satisfied, yet."

Now, Logan's voice. "Yeah. Who'd have figured that a kid like that . . ."

"His tracks run off that way," another voice cut in. "Maybe we should ride him down."

The first man's voice again, sarcastic now: "Yep. We been ridin' him down for some time now. At the rate he's been knockin' us off, we wouldn't last out the day."

"Tracks go into that thicket. If he's in there, waiting . . ."

Luther was moving more cautiously, down on his hands and knees, wanting to get a little closer, but worried about being seen. There were enough of them to fan out and surround the thicket. Since he was now on foot, they had the advantage of mobility. Maybe they'd even think of setting fire to the thicket.

It was Logan who made the final decision. "Hell," he muttered. "I ain't hot to ride into that mess. Let's get the hell outta here, like we figured before. If Stark hadn't been so all fired hot to bushwhack the son of a bitch, we'd be that much further along the trail. Let the bastard try and take us on our own ground."

Luther could hear the creak of saddle leather, the jingle of bridles and spurs as the men turned their horses around. He wanted to break cover, open fire on them, but they were still too far away, and mounted, while he was not. They'd come at him from all sides.

He listened to them go, until he could hear them no longer. He walked back to his horse. The mare was cropping some of the spare grass inside the thicket. Luther led her along, until he found a more open spot. He took a file out of his saddlebags, and used it to hammer the horseshoe nails back into the hoof. He managed to get it fairly tight, but knew it would not hold for long; one nail had broken off, another was bent and rusty.

He remembered that there was a town about twenty miles away. There'd probably be a blacksmith. He headed for the town, but was not able to reach it that day. He camped four miles short of it. The shoe had fallen off completely. The next morning he walked the final few miles, leading the mare, wearing his moccasins.

It was easy enough to get the mare reshod, but the blacksmith warned him that he'd better rest her for a couple of days. "That bad shoe put a lotta pressure on her hoof. You ride her too hard now, you're gonna end up with a lame horse, mister."

So Luther checked into the local hotel, aware that Logan and company were building up a big lead. They'd disappear into Mexico. Their trail would grow cold. He'd have a hell of a time finding them.

The morning of the third day he was off again, but moving slowly, babying the mare. If she did go lame, he'd have to get another horse. Not a pleasant thought; he was used to the mare, and she to him. He'd hate to ride an untried animal into the kind of confrontation that he figured awaited him down below the border.

He reached the Mexican line three days later. So far he'd been able to follow the tracks Logan and his bunch had left, but a little way over the border he lost them completely; there'd been too damned much traffic. Their tracks had been obliterated.

The land was dry, inhospitable. The great Sonora desert. Luther worried about water; he'd have to be careful, plan ahead, ride from one source of water to the next.

He stopped in a small village, asked people if they'd seen three gringos passing this way. It was a poor village, and its people had long ago learned to pay no attention to other people's troubles. It had been a lesson painfully learned. All Luther got was incomprehension and blank stares.

He rode in a big arc, hoping to pick up some trace of his quarry. The land was only lightly populated. Three gringos should stand out clearly, be remembered . . . if he could get anybody to talk. Luther started going into cantinas, buying drinks, loosening the locals up with booze before asking his questions. His meager Spanish began to improve.

Finally, in one village, boasting the wealth of two separate cantinas, he struck pay dirt. He'd been pouring cheap mescal down the throat of a middle-aged campesino. At least he looked middle-aged; maybe he was younger. In this harsh land, it was hard to tell.

The man looked like he spent a great deal more time in cantinas than out working. Half-drunk, he finally informed Luther that, yes, indeed, there was a gringo here. But not being a man of taste, this gringo frequented the town's other, less favored cantina.

A single gringo. Not Logan and his bunch. Well, maybe he'd know if other gringos were nearby. Luther motioned to the patron that the rest of the bottle was to remain with his informant, then he left the cantina. The other cantina was around the corner on a side street. Luther debated taking his horse. Finally, he took only the Winchester, and set out.

This second cantina was smaller, a sad little shack, half adobe, half wattle and daub. Luther leaned against the outside wall for a moment, keeping one eye shut, letting his night vision build up in that eye. Finally, he walked in through the low doorway, hating to stoop, but having no choice.

He opened his eye the moment he was inside. The interior was cramped, just one room, with a couple of sagging tables, and a plank bar. A gringo was leaning against the bar. As Luther's entry momentarily blocked the light from the doorway, the man looked up. The light was behind Luther; he was nothing but a silhouette . . . until he moved further into the room. Then the man's eyes widened, and he backed away along the bar until he reached the wall. "You!" he burst out.

Luther recognized him . . . one of the men who'd been riding with Logan. Luther glanced around the room. No one else was there but an old man, a Mexican, obviously very drunk. The front door was the only door.

The gringo was standing frozen, his eyes riveted on the muzzle of Luther's rifle . . . which was pointed at his belly. "I ain't goin' for my gun," he said tightly. "I ain't got no fight with you, mister."

The man was plainly terrified. He'd seen his companions go down one after the other at the hands of the man now facing him.

"Maybe I haven't got any fight with you, either," Luther said, his voice quiet but cold. "Maybe I just want a little information."

Then, his tone whip-crack sharp, he asked "Where's Logan and the other one?"

"Not here," the man said quickly. "They rode on. To the town where they usually hole up. I dropped out, didn't want no more part of 'em."

The man was eager to talk. Within a couple of minutes Luther had learned that the one man still with Logan was named Rafferty. "Mean as a snake," the man in the bar told Luther. "Likes killin' people just for the fun of it. I seen him kill a woman, once. I don't like ridin' with that kinda man. He an' Logan are two rattlers outta the same nest.

"And then there's these three Mexes," the man continued, more at ease now. "They're kinda in with Logan. He gives 'em money from time to time. They keep the town quiet, take care of anybody local who tries to get in Logan's way. Those three greasers are real banditos. They'd kill their own mother for a drink of tequila."

Luther nodded, started backing away toward the door. "I'm leaving now," he said. "If I see you poke your head outside, I'll blow it off."

The man nodded. "It ain't my fight, mister."

Luther backed out into the street, then walked around the corner and headed for his horse. He doubted the man would make any effort to warn Logan; he seemed thoroughly sick of that bunch. But to make sure he got to Logan first, Luther decided to ride straight toward the other village.

It was only a two-hour ride. He reached the town in the middle of the afternoon. Both he and his horse were drooping from the oven-like heat. He knew he should rest a while, but he decided to ride straight on in, before somebody spotted him.

There was a cantina on the main street. Luther tied up his horse out front, and went inside, taking the Winchester with him. He went in with the rifle's muzzle covering the room, ready to start shooting if he saw Logan or any of his bunch.

But there were no gringos inside, just a few older men, obviously dirt-poor campesinos. There was also a younger Mexican, and a young woman. Everyone noticed the rifle straight off. Everyone froze . . . until Luther lowered the muzzle. The girl had been standing near the younger man. She looked up at Luther. "*Señor?*" she said, a question in her voice.

She must be the barmaid. "*Una cerveza,*" Luther replied, through a very dry throat.

She nodded, then went behind the bar. Luther noticed that she walked with a lot of extra movement. He was sure that she was very aware of him looking at her. He watched as she reached below the bar, then brought up a bottle, which she put on top of the bar's warped and dirty surface. Luther continued watching as she opened the bottle. She was starting to reach for one of the dirty glasses behind the bar, of which there were very few, when Luther picked up the bottle, tipped it back, and poured a flood of beer down his throat. It was not very cool, but it tasted wonderful.

Luther began to pay more attention to the others in the bar. Or rather, to the younger man, who was the only one worth noticing. He was in his late twenties, fairly good-sized, and as evil-looking an hombre as Luther had ever seen, with a big drooping moustache, lank, greasy hair, close-set eyes, which were very black, and a mouth that had set into a perpetual leer.

The girl came around the edge of the bar. Luther spent a second or two on a further appraisal. She was a little battered-looking, but still attractive, perhaps twenty or twenty-two years old, which in this area meant she was on the verge of middle age. Her best feature was her hair, long, and black, and shining. Her low-cut blouse indicated a couple of other pleasing features. She was eyeing Luther speculatively. Which the hard-looking Mexican noticed. "*Venga,*" he snarled, pulling her toward him. She started to resist, to pull away. The Mexican casually cuffed her across the side of the head, then pulled her close against him. One of his hands slid down beneath the top of her blouse and began kneading. He must have pinched hard, because the girl's face twisted with pain, and she gave a little yelp.

"Let her go," Luther said in English, and when the man did not respond, he repeated it in Spanish. The man grinned. His hand worked harder. The girl let out a louder cry of pain.

Luther had leaned his rifle against the bar when he'd started drinking his beer. He took a step toward the Mexican and the girl. He had not noticed a gun on the man, only a knife in a sheath. The Mexican, still grinning, pulled out the knife, and laid the edge against the girl's throat. Luther stopped. He wondered if he could draw his pistol and kill the man before he cut the girl. Maybe, maybe not. What he did know was that he could not abide a man who misused a woman. It didn't matter to him whether that woman was a duchess, or a ragged barmaid in a run-down Mexican cantina.

The Mexican's smile faded a little when Luther drew his pistol. He watched attentively as Luther placed the pistol on the bar. His smile returned when Luther pulled out his own knife, and stood waiting, in the middle of the room, legs spread apart a little for balance. "Come on, *cabrón*," Luther said quietly. "Try that knife on a man."

The Mexican let go of the girl, shoved her against the bar. He too moved toward the middle of the room. The cantina's other occupants scattered, some running out the door. "I think I know somebody who is looking for a man of your description, gringo," the Mexican said, leering even more broadly. "He'll give me lots of money when I take him your head."

Luther and the Mexican began to circle one another . . . as much as they could within the cramped confines of the cantina. It was the Mexican who made the first move, lunging at Luther, then changing from a lunge to a cut, a short arcing slice that brushed Luther's sleeve, cutting the material, but only grazing the flesh beneath.

Luther leaped backward. He instantly noticed that the Mexican was off balance. Now Luther moved, straight ahead, cutting with the huge blade. The Mexican tried to block with his knife, but his blade was too light. Blade pressing against blade, the Mexican's hand was forced down. Luther pressed harder, working the point of his knife almost an inch into the flesh on the wrist of the Mexican's knife hand.

The Mexican swore, backed away, stumbling a little as Luther drove on after him. Luther cut hard, twice. One cut opened a deep wound six inches long on the Mexican's left forearm, the second cut, swooping low, sliced deep into his thigh.

Blood was pouring from the Mexican's arm and leg. The feel of warm wetness running out of his own body, the knowledge that he was cut so badly that he would soon weaken from loss of blood, forced the Mexican to lunge forward recklessly, thrusting at Luther's throat. Luther parried the blow with his left hand, guiding the blade past his face. Stepping in close, he buried his own blade deep in the other man's stomach.

The Mexican uttered a guttural grunt, a sound more of amazement than of pain. He'd killed a number of men with his knife; he had never imagined that he'd have another man's knife in his own belly.

And then the pain came . . . as Luther ripped his knife sideways, opening a huge gash in the Mexican's stomach. The Mexican screamed, doubled up, backed away, his knife falling onto the floor as he pressed both hands to his belly in a vain effort to halt the huge rush of blood pouring from between his shaking fingers.

Luther stepped back, avoiding the blood. There was clearly no fight left in the man, but he was worried about the scream. It might bring the person the Mexican had mentioned, the one looking for a man like Luther. No doubt that'd be Logan.

Suddenly a gunshot roared from behind Luther. He spun around, his knife ready, cursing himself for moving so far away from his pistol. And then he saw it . . . in the hands of the girl. She was holding it clumsily in front of her. Smoke was trickling from the pistol's barrel, but it was not pointed at Luther. "*Cerdo!*" she hissed, looking past Luther. "Pig!"

He took the pistol from her, then turned. She'd shot the Mexican in the belly, just a few inches above the knife wound. The Mexican was clutching at the bar now, starting to go down, his face slack, his eyes staring at the girl.

Luther paid him no more attention. The shot would have been heard all over town. He looked around the cantina. There was only one old man left inside. Perhaps one of the others was already on his way to spread the news about the newcomer. Maybe spread it to Tom Logan.

Luther shucked the empty from his pistol, replaced it with a fresh load, then reholstered the pistol. He looked over at the girl. She was beginning to shake now, either from fear, or from a simple physical reaction to what she had just done. She looked around wildly, caught sight of Luther. "The others," she said. "They will take me, and . . ."

Her voice faded away. "What others?" Luther asked. She did not seem to hear him, she was looking at the Mexican again, who was lying motionless on the floor in a huge pool of blood. Luther moved directly in front of the girl, took her chin in his hand, looked her straight in the face. "What others?" he demanded.

Her eyes cleared a little. "Two more like this pig," she said, pointing at the dead Mexican. "And two gringos. Bad men, all of them."

Luther nodded, then picked up his rifle and raced for the door. He did not want to be caught in a place with only one exit. He was barely clear of the door when he heard a shout, someone calling out in Spanish. He turned. Two hard-looking Mexicans, of the same type as the man he'd gutted in the bar, real banditos, were running toward him. One was carrying a rifle; it looked like an old Henry. The other was wearing crossed gun belts, drawing a pistol with his right hand. Another pistol rode on his left hip.

Luther turned away, running behind the cantina. He heard a shot. A bullet gouged adobe a foot from his head. He heard more yelling, then the sound of someone running. They were coming after him.

He sprinted across a little open area. Two dilapidated shacks lay ahead. They had thick adobe walls, only about waist-high in some places; the roofs had long ago fallen in.

He ran behind one of the adobe walls. He couldn't believe his luck when one of his pursuers came bulling his way around the corner of the cantina. The one with the pistols. There he was, right out in the open, an easy target. Half-hidden behind the wall, Luther opened fire with the Winchester, three evenly spaced shots. He hit the Mexican with all three bullets. The first stopped him as if he'd run into a tree, the second and third drove him backward. He fell hard, and did not move again.

The second Mexican was a little more careful. He came around the far side of the cantina, so that the corner of one thick wall protected him. He opened fire with his rifle. Good accurate fire, which forced Luther down behind the wall.

Luther heard more shouting, this time in English. A man poked his head around the side of the cantina. Luther popped up, fired a quick shot, had a momentary image of Logan's surprised face as Luther's bullet drove adobe chips in his direction.

Then Luther had to duck down again, as the Mexican on the far side of the cantina got off two more shots. Things were getting hotter than Luther cared for. If he didn't get on the move, they'd box him in.

It was easy leaving the ruined house; the whole back wall was gone. Luther ducked behind another house further along. Then he heard Logan, calling out, "Hey! Is that you, kid?"

Luther did not reply, but worked his way further behind the house. Logan and the Mexican had not made any move to follow him. Which Luther did not like. How many other men did Logan have? The gunman Luther had questioned in that other town had told him about three Mexicans and somebody named Rafferty. The girl in the bar had mentioned two surviving Mexicans and two white men. Counting the Mexican Luther had just shot, that should leave Logan, Rafferty, and one Mexican.

He knew where the Mexican was. And Logan. But where the hell was Rafferty?

Logan was still calling out. "We're gonna get you, kid. We got you boxed in. Comin' into our town was a stupid move. We know every hidin' place."

Luther moved around to the side, slipping from cover to cover. He could see them now, about fifty yards away, Logan and the Mexican, half-hidden behind the cantina, still facing the ruins where Luther had been hiding earlier. Obviously, they had not seen him slip away. He brought up his rifle, but he could not see enough of his targets. He'd have to get closer, move further around to the side, pin them against the wall of the building.

He was halfway to the cantina before they saw him. Logan had just motioned for the Mexican to run toward the side of a building about twenty yards from the ruin. The Mexican violently shook his head. Luther could see Logan pointing, scowling. The Mexican, still shaking his head, gave in. Luther saw him go into a crouch, ready to run for the cover Logan had indicated.

Then Logan spotted Luther. "There he is!" Logan shouted. He was carrying only a pistol. He raised it, got off a shot. The Mexican, startled, was late in turning, fighting to bring the long barrel of his rifle around.

Luther opened up on the Mexican; he was the only one with a rifle, so he was the most dangerous. Luther put two shots into the man, then turned his rifle onto Logan, just as Logan fired again. Both men shot too quickly. Both missed, but the bullets came close enough to drive both men behind cover.

Luther could hear the sound of Logan's boot heels, pounding along the street. He was headed for somewhere, and as he'd said, he knew this town. Luther didn't. And where the hell was Rafferty? Would he step out of hiding somewhere, and gun Luther down?

Following the sound of Logan's boots, Luther began to run along the sides of buildings, keeping in their shadow, ready to hit the ground if anybody opened up on him. Then he caught sight of Logan, running toward the largest building in town. The church. Luther fired and missed, just as Logan ducked into the church door.

Damn. He'd be hard to get at now. The church walls were at least three feet thick, and Luther had no idea how the interior of

the church was laid out. In addition, he had to protect his back
from Rafferty. If the man was even here.

Luther settled down under good cover, facing the church's front
door. A minute passed. Then another. Luther was figuring he
would have to find some way to get inside the church, when
Logan called out again. "Hey, kid!" he shouted, from just inside
the church's door. "It's just me an' you now. You son of a bitch,
you killed all my men. Just you an' me left. So why don't we
settle it, face-to-face, like men? Just the two of us. Out in the
open. With pistols."

Luther felt a surge of elation. Finally, he would be able to face
the last of the men who'd killed Jedadiah. Able to look right into
Logan's eyes as he opened fire. Logan was the worst. He was the
one who'd claimed friendship with Jedadiah, then murdered him.
For gold. For profit.

Luther was about to step out into the street, ready to take Logan
up on his offer, when he thought again. Uh-uh. The man who'd
so treacherously killed Jedadiah was not the kind of man who'd
make a genuine offer to face Luther in a fair fight. He'd have
some kind of trick up his sleeve. And that trick probably had a
name. Rafferty.

There was movement by the church door. It was Logan, stepping outside, then ducking behind a high wall. "I'm out in the
open now," Logan shouted. "You step on out, too. We'll both
walk down the street toward one another. Then have it out."

Brave, honest words. From a man Luther knew was anything
but brave and honest. But where was the trick?

Luther quickly scanned the area. The street was lined with
adobe houses, most with blank front walls broken only by heavy
doors. No windows. No place at all for a bushwhacker to hide.

Then Luther looked up, toward the top of the church. The bell
tower. He studied the tower for a moment, was about to look
away again, then saw a flicker of movement, a glint of sunlight
off metal.

Rafferty. He'd never met the man, but it had to be Rafferty. He
was up in the bell tower with a rifle. Had to be him. It was a setup.
As soon as Luther stepped out into the street for the showdown
with Logan, Rafferty would shoot him from the church tower.
Logan and Rafferty had probably set this whole thing up as soon
as they realized trouble had come to town.

Luther studied the tower. He could see at least one bell up there.
It was hard to see inside the tower; the part facing the street had a

high wall screening the bells. But on the left side, the whole top of the tower was open.

"Okay," Luther shouted to Logan. "I'm coming out into the street. But I'm gonna hang onto my rifle until I see you in the open."

By calling out, he had indicated his position. And now he changed that position, running silently to his left, where he would be able to see the side of the church. He caught movement down the street, Logan walking out into the open, secure in the knowledge that Rafferty was there to cover him. "Hey, kid, where the hell are you?" Logan shouted, an edge of nervousness in his voice.

Luther took cover behind a wall only about thirty yards from the side of the church. It was a rather squat church, with a squat bell tower, and now Luther was looking straight into the tower. Straight at Rafferty, who was facing the street, in profile to Luther, with a rifle in his hands, ready to stand and open fire the moment Luther came out into the open.

But it was Luther who opened fire, levering a dozen quick rounds into the bell tower, a flurry of lead. Bullets pinged off the bells, ricocheted from the stone walls, zigzagged throughout the tower. Several of them, partially flattened from contact with the bells and the stone, tore into Rafferty's body. Luther saw Rafferty spin around inside the tower, his rifle falling out the embrasure into the street. For a moment he clutched hold of the rope that rang the bells, and as he hung there, the bells started ringing loudly. Then Rafferty lost his grip, and fell out the side of the tower.

Luther heard him hit the ground, but by then he was already racing back toward the street. Logan was still out in the open, staring stupidly up at the tower. He did not see Luther at first. "Logan!" Luther called out. "Now it really is just you and me."

Logan spun, saw Luther. He turned and began to run, but there was no place to go. He tried the door of the church first, but someone had closed it from the inside. Logan ran to his right, stopped at a door and pounded on it frantically. The door did not open.

Luther continued to walk toward Logan. When only thirty yards separated them, Logan had no choice but to turn and face Luther. His face was working, first with fear, then with a growing animal rage. "You son of a bitch!" he screamed. "You been doggin' my trail for too damned long. Now you're gonna die!"

Having worked himself into a rage, Logan drew his pistol. And in his rage, opened fire. But anger had unsteadied his hand. Three shots flew by Luther before he had his own pistol leveled. The range was considerable for six-shooters, thirty yards. Luther held the pistol in both hands, sighted carefully, and fired one shot.

The bullet took Logan in the middle of his chest, knocking him flat on his back. His pistol hit the ground a yard from his hand. Luther walked up to where Logan lay, his pistol cocked, ready to fire again.

But Logan was dead. Luther stood over the body, shifting his weight from foot to foot, confused. It had ended so quickly. Two years of hunting Jedadiah's killers, Harrington dead so long ago he could barely remember killing him, the hard fighting, whittling down Logan's bunch, Stark dead days ago, and now it was all over with a single shot.

And he felt nothing. Nothing at all.

CHAPTER EIGHTEEN

Luther left the village immediately, left the bodies where they lay. As he passed the cantina, riding out of town, he caught sight of the cantina girl's face just inside the doorway. She started to duck back inside. He stopped his horse. "They're dead," he said in Spanish.

She moved a step forward, her face incredulous. But she had heard the firing, and Luther was still alive, so it must be true. "*Gracias a Dios!*" she burst out, smiling joyfully.

Luther nudged his horse into motion again. He turned once, just after passing the last house in the village. People were coming out into the street, clearly excited. The girl from the cantina was walking back and forth, talking, gesticulating. Everyone looked very happy. Apparently Logan and his men had not been popular.

Luther rode on. He knew that he should be feeling good, like the villagers. He'd come to the end of a long trail . . . only to find himself on the beginning of another.

Fife. Duncan Fife. The man who'd killed his father. Because of his promise to Jedadiah, Luther had put off his reckoning with Fife. Now he could put it off no longer.

Fife, however, was a different kettle of fish than Jedadiah's killers. Luther had just wiped out an outlaw gang; there would be no trouble with the law over that. Sure, he had that old charge against him for maiming that crooked sheriff, but no one had seemed very serious about making the charge stick.

However, Duncan Fife . . . killing him would have very different results. Fife was wealthy, an important man, he had connections in Washington. He was an owner, a boss, a man of power.

His death would put Luther squarely on the wrong side of the law. They'd never stop looking for him.

Of course, he could simply bushwhack Fife, pot him with the Sharps from ambush, then ride away, unseen. Luther's stomach recoiled at the thought. He was no back-shooter. But what was he going to do? The odds were so against him. Fife would be surrounded by guards, by a whole mine full of men.

Luther decided to put the matter out of his mind. Just . . . ride. He was vaguely aware that he was heading north, always north. Toward Colorado. And the mine. He rode, he ate, he slept. He tried not to think at all. Finally, one day, he realized that he was just a few miles from Jedadiah's cabin . . . what had been Jedadiah's cabin. On impulse he turned his horse in that direction. Immediately, the landscape began to look familiar. There were memories, now, of covering this same area on foot, with Jedadiah alongside him, pointing out this and that, making Luther aware of features, dangers, advantages, that his untrained boy's mind would never have noticed.

He was no longer an untrained boy. Now he noticed everything that moved, and most that didn't . . . effortlessly. His mind automatically picked out possible places of ambush, assessed the landscape for defensive and offensive positions. He heard every sound, tested the air for scents that should or should not be there.

Today, everything was as it should be. He rode over a little hill. Jedadiah's cabin lay two hundreds yards ahead, planted solidly on the ground. He had half-expected it to be a ruin, the roof fallen in, varmints living where Jedadiah had lived, but it appeared to be in good shape, as if someone had been taking care of it.

Aware that, here in these mountains, riding right up to a man's front door was a good way to get shot, Luther stopped fifty yards away, then sang out a loud halloo.

There was no answer. Luther rode up to the door and dismounted. The door was closed from the outside, a dowel thrust through a wooden hasp. So the cabin must be empty. Luther examined the dowel. It looked like the same one he'd left there himself, over two years ago, perhaps a little more worn, but with the same odd bulge at one end.

He removed the dowel, then pushed the door open. He could see little of the inside; it was too late in the day for light to penetrate deeply. With his hand on the butt of his Colt, he stepped inside, automatically moving to the side, so that he would not be framed in the doorway.

The place felt empty. As his eyes adjusted to the gloom, Luther noticed a lantern on the table. He walked over, struck a match, and lit the lantern. There was plenty of oil; the wick burned brightly.

The cabin was pretty much as he had left it. Maybe a little cleaner. There was a note tacked onto one wall. The note read, "Gone to California. Use the place, but clean it up for the next pilgrim who passes by."

So, the cabin had provided shelter, for someone who had taken good care of it. Fine. Now it would provide shelter for Luther. He felt as if he were home.

Luther spent two weeks in the cabin, resting, starting to think again. Once, just once, he walked up to the place where he'd buried Jedadiah. The grave was still intact, nothing had gotten into it.

He roamed the hills, on foot. He'd replaced the moccasins Jedadiah had made with a pair he'd bought from a Blackfoot Indian. He brought down a deer, and smoked the meat into jerky. Most of it he hung from the cabin's rafters. There was enough for a long time, longer than he'd be here . . . because he had finally decided. His youth had not been quite totally redeemed. There was still that one loose end to tie up. Fife. He was going after Duncan Fife. Going right in for the kill. No more two year hunts. He'd go straight for Fife. Within days, either Fife would be dead . . . or Luther would.

The next morning Luther once again slipped the dowel into the hasp. A final look around, then he mounted and rode his horse away from the cabin. He stopped at the crest of a hill, looked back just once, then rode on. Toward the mine.

The mine was less than a day's ride. Luther had thought of stopping along the way, camping for the night, then riding in next morning. He decided not to wait, but to go in now, get it done.

As before, when he and his father had been slogging along on foot, he felt the effects of the mine long before he saw it, heard the heavy thud of the stamp mill, saw the cloud of dust and smoke ahead, smelled the stench of the place. Finally, he reached the hilltop from which he and his father had first looked down on the mine, over three years ago. Sickness knotted his guts as he remembered how it had been, the helplessness of the men who worked for Duncan Fife, the pain of watching his father age in front of him, recognition of the increasing danger. And finally, his father's death, his own beating, Fife's goons leaving him for dead in the snow.

But he'd been a boy then. He was a boy no longer. As Logan and Stark and the men with them had discovered, Luther had become a highly efficient killing machine.

He pushed fear way into the back of his mind, leaving just enough to keep him alert. He rode down into the valley, toward the mine buildings, all his senses awake, sharpened. As Jedadiah had once told him, when the chips are down you have to see with your ears, hear with your eyes, turn your entire body into a single sense organ.

He was now riding past some of the miners' shacks. Men stood in doorways. A few of them looked up, saw a tall man with icy cold eyes, heavily armed. They instinctively shrank away.

Luther's gaze ranged everywhere, checking buildings, alleyways, looking ahead for possible trouble, seeing everything.

A man stepped out of a cabin, saw Luther, started to step back. "Mr. Jackson!" Luther called out. "Homer Jackson!"

The man stopped just outside the doorway. He appeared puzzled, as if he almost recognized Luther, but was not quite certain. "Luther McCall," Luther said, stopping his horse a few feet away.

The man's mouth sagged. "Luther?" he finally managed to say. "Horace's boy?"

"The same."

"But we thought . . . we thought . . ."

Suddenly Homer gestured. "Get on down," he said quickly. "Get outta sight. If they see you . . ."

Luther took a long look around. He saw no immediate danger, so he dismounted, but kept his horse's reins in his left hand. Homer was still looking around nervously, moving further into the doorway. "Come on inside," he insisted.

Luther tied his horse to a post in front of the door, then took his Winchester from its saddle scabbard. He followed Homer into the shack. Inside, it was a miserable place, as miserable as the shack Luther and his father had lived in. Horace gestured toward a chair. Luther looked around, saw no reason not to sit, so he did.

Homer sat opposite him. "We thought . . ." he started to say.

"Thought what?" Luther asked. "What were you told about me?"

"Well, nothin', really. Just your place burnin' down, an' you disappearin'. Well, we figured they done you in. Dumped you somewhere for the vultures and coyotes."

"They tried," Luther said flatly. "I survived."

"Yeah. I can see that. But, hell, I hardly recognized ya. You look, well . . . different."

"And the mine?" Luther asked. "What's happening here at the mine?"

"Well," Homer said, clearing his throat. For the next half hour he filled Luther in on the local situation. It had not changed much. Fife still employed thugs to maintain discipline, he still paid low wages, and men still died because of the lack of safety precautions. "Since your father, uh, died," Homer explained, "Fife's had it pretty much his own way. Particularly after you . . . disappeared. But there *has* been some, well, payin' back. You remember those four goons, the ones that were there when your father, well, fell down the shaft? Two of 'em had more or less the same kinda accidents. One fell, the other got killed when a charge went off prematurely."

"And the other two?" Luther asked.

"Still here. Still makin' life miserable for the rest of us. You probably remember 'em. Tarkington and Bates."

Luther shifted in the chair, ran his hand over the stock of his rifle. Yes, he remembered Tarkington and Bates. Had forgotten their names, but knew he'd never forget their faces. "Where can I find them?" he asked.

Homer looked shocked. "You don't mean you're gonna . . . ?"

"I'm going to kill them. And Fife, too."

The words were said flatly, in so unemotional a voice that Homer felt a chill run through him. Then, as he looked into Luther's eyes, he wondered if he felt chilled for Luther, or for Fife and his thugs. "There's six of 'em now," he said hastily. "Fife hired himself a top gun hand, up from Texas, name of Pearson. Mean son of a bitch. Then there's the two you're after, and three more. All tough hombres. They carry guns."

Luther nodded absently. Not the best of odds. But then, Logan had started after him with more than a dozen men. Most of whom were now dead. Of course, Luther had had plenty of open space in which to maneuver. The mine area was very congested. Maybe he could make that congestion work for him. "Where can I find the men I'm after?" he asked. "And where's Fife?"

"Well," Homer said, "Fife still has his place up behind the mine offices. As for the others, some are gonna be on duty, some not. You'd just have to . . . find 'em."

Luther stood up. "That's what I'll do."

Homer stood up, too. "But that's crazy, kid . . . Luther. There's too many. And there's a telegraph here now. Fife could just call for the law. . . ."

"I don't think he will. Not right away."

Luther was already heading for the door. He turned just before leaving. "Warn the men," he said to Homer. "Tell 'em to keep out of the way. There'll probably be a lot of shooting."

When he was out in the street again, he reached into his saddlebags, pulled out his cartridge pouch, and slung it over his shoulder. He started to mount, then decided that his horse would probably be safer here. And worse than useless in the warren of narrow alleys around the mine buildings.

He walked straight to the mine offices, then right through the front door. The same clerk who had hired his father was sitting in the same chair, behind the same desk. He looked up in irritation as Luther entered. "Yes?" he started to say, then took a closer look at Luther. "Hey! You can't bring guns in here. . . ."

Anger surged through Luther. Cold anger. The clerk was just as arrogant, just as supercilious as he'd been before. Just as condescending. Luther pointed the rifle at him, and pulled back the hammer. The clerk paled. "What? What?" he stammered, his eyes riveted on the rifle's muzzle.

"Where's Duncan Fife?" Luther asked coldly.

"Why . . . why . . . inspecting the stamp mill, or the mine. I don't know which. I haven't seen him for several . . ."

"And Bates and Tarkington," Luther continued. "Two of the guards."

"Well," the clerk stammered, "Mr. Tarkington is on patrol. I don't know about Mr. Bates. . . ."

Luther walked closer to the clerk. "I want you out of here," he said. "I want you out in the streets. I want you to carry the word . . . that the only ones I'm after are Bates, Tarkington, and Duncan Fife. I won't bother anybody else . . . unless they bother me."

He leaned closer to the clerk. "Do you understand what I've said?"

The muzzle of the Winchester was only inches from the clerk's belly. He swallowed once, then managed to croak out a yes.

"Then get out in the street. Pass the word."

Luther started to turn away. The clerk managed to blurt out, "But why? What do you want with those men?"

Luther turned back, surprise on his face. "Why . . . I'm going to kill them."

Seeing the shocked look on the clerk's face, he added, "You tell them that Luther McCall has come back. Luther McCall. Horace McCall's boy."

Recognition flooded the clerk's eyes. "Oh God!" he blurted, as he watched Luther walk out the door. Then he, too, left, ran out the back door, heading for the building where the guards lived.

CHAPTER NINETEEN

Out in the street, Luther glanced around quickly, to see if anything had changed in the last few years. Not much had; there were still the same filthy, muck-strewn, muddy alleys, running between rows of sagging wooden buildings. The alleys were narrow, with lots of openings angling off in every direction. There were plenty of places for a single man, chased by many men, to hide, to circle around, to surprise his pursuers.

Luther heard yelling from further uphill; probably the clerk warning the guards. If they were worth their salt, they'd be after him in a couple of minutes. He hoped the clerk had delivered his warning . . . that he was only after Fife, Tarkington, and Bates. He doubted it would do any good, and he did not particularly care if any of them got killed. They were guards. Company goons. Mercenaries, oppressing their fellow workingmen. For blood money. Whatever they got, they deserved.

Luther was just starting for an even narrower alleyway when a man came into view. A big man, carrying a shotgun. The man was Tarkington, one of the guards who'd killed Luther's father. Luther recognized him easily, remembered the expression of pleasure on Tarkington's face as he had stood over Luther, beating him.

Tarkington stopped, stood spraddle-legged, the shotgun leaning against his shoulder. "Hey, you!" he shouted. "What the hell are you doin' with that rifle?"

Apparently Tarkington had not yet heard the news. Now he became aware of the shouting coming from further up the slope, near the company headquarters. He looked puzzled for a moment, looked away, then back at Luther. "Are you the reason for all that ruckus?" he asked truculently.

His shotgun swung down, covering Luther. "Yeah," Luther called out. "What's the matter, Tarkington? Don't you remember me?"

"Huh?" Tarkington grunted, looking puzzled. "How come you know my name?"

"Try and remember, Tarkington. Lots of snow. A burning shack. Beating up a boy, leaving him to die. Pushing a good man down a mine shaft."

Tarkington's face went blank for a moment, then came alive as he began to remember. "You? But you were . . ."

"Luther McCall, Tarkington. Come back to send you to hell."

"Says who, you son of a bitch?" Tarkington snarled, all action now. The shotgun, which had wavered for a moment, came back up into line. Luther let it track right onto him, tried to sense that exact moment when Tarkington would fire, and at that moment Luther spun to his right, just a few feet, but it was enough.

Since he was already pressing the trigger, Tarkington did not have time to correct. The load of buckshot tore through the space where Luther had been just moments before. One pellet nicked him in the side, breaking the skin, but the butt of Luther's Winchester was already against his shoulder. He fired, hit Tarkington in the solar plexus. With a huge "Whoof!" Tarkington flew backward, the shotgun flying from his grip, landing next to an alleyway.

Tarkington was still on his feet; he'd staggered back against the side of a building. He stood for a moment, looking down at the shotgun. Luther was already running forward, closing the distance. Tarkington was holding his stomach with his left hand, his face pasty white. He shuffled a half step toward the shotgun, but Luther was now only six feet away. He raised his rifle, aimed it directly at Tarkington's face. "For my father," Luther said quietly, then blew Tarkington's head off.

Of course, the shooting was bound to attract trouble. Luther heard angry shouting, then footsteps pounding in his direction. It must be the guards. Luther looked around quickly, saw movement at the mouth of an alley, brought up the Winchester, then lowered it again. It was Homer Jackson. "I've been passing the word," Homer called out softly.

Luther nodded, ducked into an alleyway, began to walk rapidly between buildings. The shouting behind him grew louder.

He could tell, by the cursing, when they found Tarkington's body. "Son of a bitch!" someone snarled. "The bastard killed ol' Jake."

Then another voice, sharp with authority. "Where the hell's his shotgun?"

"Sombitch musta taken it."

"Well, hell," the authoritative voice snapped. "Let's get after him. We'll spread out, circle around the area, pin him down."

Must be the chief guard, Luther decided. He sounded cool, competent. Too damned competent. Luther hadn't had a chance to do his own circling yet, and now they were going to throw out a net.

Then another voice cut in. A high-pitched, angry voice. "What's goin' on here, you men? What were all that shootin' aboot?"

Duncan Fife. Luther had not heard that voice for years, but he easily recognized it, remembered its petulant, hectoring tone, would recognize it in a crowded place from a hundred yards away.

"Some yahoo named McCall, Mr. Fife," the guard captain said. "Came into the office, bold as brass, said he was here to kill you, and two of my men. Looks like he already got one."

Luther moved quickly, starting to swing around in a big arc, cutting through narrow alleyways. He heard Fife say, after a moment of dead silence, the mine owner's voice choked, "McCall? But . . . but, he fell down the mine shaft, years ago. I . . . we had a funeral."

Now the clerk's voice: "His son, Mr. Fife. Luther McCall. He came into the office. . . ."

"Whaaat?" A shriek from Fife, a wail of incredulity. "But . . ."

Then, Fife's voice again, babbling now: "Get after him! Find him. Kill him!"

"Yessir."

The sound of men running. But Fife's interference had slowed them down just long enough for Luther to get into position. He figured he was now outside any perimeter. He'd be the one who had the others boxed in. A moment later a man carrying a shotgun came into view, running hard. Luther stepped out of his hiding place. "I only want Bates and Fife," he called out. "You . . ."

But the man, hearing Luther's voice, spun, bringing his shotgun up high. Luther shot him twice, first in the leg, then, after he fell, in the right shoulder. The man had dropped his shotgun. "Don't!" he called out as Luther aimed at him again. "Don't shoot me no more!"

Luther nodded, then began running, heading down another alley. He heard yelling from behind him. Someone had found the man he shot, and now was calling out, drawing others in that direction. Good. They'd bunch up, then he could . . .

But one man had separated himself from the pack. Luther caught sight of him a moment before the man opened fire, not with a shotgun, but with a Winchester. Luther barely had time to duck around a corner. The man called out—Luther recognized his voice, it was the guard captain—"I got him pinned down behind the mess hall, boys. Come around behind him, and we'll finish off the bastard."

Too damned right, Luther thought. The guard captain, probably the only real professional among a pack of thugs, had kept his cool, had made a wider loop than Luther had expected . . . and now had Luther trapped between himself and the others.

It would have to be a face-to-face fight, rifle against rifle. Luther sprinted forward, toward the cover of another building. The guard captain fired twice. One bullet missed completely, the other dug a shallow furrow through the flesh of Luther's left forearm.

Now the guard captain broke cover, believing Luther would continue running down the alley, but Luther surprised him, by popping partway out into the open. He leaned against the side of the building for stability, then opened fire, just a shade more quickly than the guard captain.

Luther's bullet hit the guard captain low in the right side. The man staggered, but managed to fire back. His bullet plowed into the side of the building, driving wood splinters through Luther's shirt. Luther fired two more times. His first bullet missed, the second hit the guard captain in the throat, just as he levered another round into his Winchester. Blood sprayed. The guard captain dropped his rifle, clutched at his throat. Luther could hear him gagging, knew that he was as good as dead.

And that he'd be dead, too, if he didn't get the hell out of there. He ran past the guard captain, who was down on his knees now, his eyes full of the terror of death. Just before disappearing around the corner of a building, Luther looked back. The guard captain had fallen forward onto his face, his body convulsing as he tried to draw air in through his ruined throat.

More swearing from behind him as the other guards discovered the guard captain's body. One man called out, "Jesus, whoever it is, he's gonna kill us all!"

Luther spun a tighter circle, coming in more quickly this time, suspecting that the remaining guards would probably be spooked. Luther intended to work his way toward the mine headquarters, where he figured he'd find Duncan Fife. If he got to Fife, and wiped him out, perhaps the guards would lose the last of their courage.

But Luther's determination to go after Fife got sidetracked when he saw another guard dart across the mouth of an alley. In that one fleeting glimpse, Luther was certain that the man was Bates, the last surviving member of the goon squad who'd pushed his father down the mine shaft.

Forgetting caution, Luther sprinted after Bates. He caught sight of him again, at the mouth of another alley. And Bates saw Luther. One frozen moment, while Luther was bringing up his rifle, then Bates, terrified, not willing to stand up to even odds, face-to-face, ducked down the alley.

Luther followed, trying to remember how this part of the mine camp was laid out. He was pretty sure there was a dead end ahead, where he would be able to pin Bates against a huge pile of mine tailings. There! Another glimpse of Bates, about forty yards ahead, ducking inside what looked like a toolshed.

Luther was so intent on Bates that he forgot to watch his own back, was not aware that one of the guards had gotten around behind him . . . until he heard the man cock both hammers of his shotgun. Luther started to spin around, moved too quickly, caught the barrel of his rifle on a sagging door, knew he wasn't going to make it, knew the man, who was only a few yards away, was about to splatter him all over the alley. Saw the grin on the guard's face.

Luther heard the blast of a shotgun. The man flew sideways, most of his head and half of one shoulder blown completely away. His shotgun spun from his hand and hit the ground. One barrel discharged, scattering mud.

Homer Jackson stepped out of an alley, holding a shotgun. "When you shot Tarkington, I . . . well . . ."

"Thanks, Homer," Luther said. "He had me cold."

Homer was having difficulty talking; his voice kept choking off. After an obvious struggle with his emotions, he started over again, under better control. "After you killed Tarkington, I picked up his shotgun, took some cartridges from his pocket. . . ."

"Load that empty barrel," Luther told him.

"Yeah, sure. Is there anything . . . ?"

"Cover my back. I'm going after another one. There can't be many left."

"No. Only a couple. But I think I saw Fife go into the telegraph office. He's probably wiring for help. . . ."

"Let him," Luther snapped. "Maybe you should go over there, keep an eye on the place."

"And you?"

Luther motioned toward the toolshed. "Bates. He's in there. He comes first."

Homer nodded, walked away, broke the shotgun open, slipped another shell into the empty barrel. Luther started down the alley toward the toolshed. He knew he'd have to be careful. Bates would be like a cornered rat. And cornered rats bite.

A quick check showed that the toolshed had no rear door, and the one window, on the far side, was too small for a man to crawl through. So Bates had to be inside.

Luther walked, light-footed, right up to the door. Standing to one side of the doorway, he thumped the butt of his Winchester hard against the wood, then immediately pulled it out of the way. Barely in time. Buckshot from both barrels of a ten-gauge shotgun blew a huge hole in the flimsy door; if Luther had been standing in front of it, he'd have been blown nearly in two.

Now he stepped directly in front of the doorway. He heard the action of a shotgun opening, the "thunk" of cartridges sliding into the huge barrels. Luther opened fire, spraying the interior of the little shed with a dozen .44 caliber slugs.

He moved out of the way again, shoving more cartridges into the Winchester's loading gate. He heard a shuffling sound. The ruined door opened. Bates staggered out, dead on his feet, the front of his body shredded by bullets. Luther was about to raise the Winchester, but Bates fell full-length on his face. One final shudder, a sigh of escaping breath, and he was dead.

Luther turned, raced back toward the mine offices. He was still fifty yards away when he heard Fife's voice, shouting, angry. "You men canna pull out now! I paid ya fer protection. If ya leave here, I'll see ya never work agin!"

A voice answered, "You hired us to baby-sit some miners, Mr. Fife. Not to go up against a one-man army. He already warned us . . . he's just after you. And some men he has a grudge against. That ain't us."

Luther could see them now, only two men left, facing Fife. They saw Luther at the same time. "Christ!" one of them burst out. He made a big show of dropping his shotgun. "We got no quarrel with you, mister," he called out. Then he walked away. The other man hesitated for a moment, then followed.

Fife stood frozen, watching them go. His face began to work spasmodically. "Traitors!" he screamed. Suddenly a pistol was in his hand. He raised it, fired twice after the two men. One screamed, arched his back, tried to reach the wound between his shoulder blades. The other, hit in the arm, staggered to safety behind a building.

Fife spun toward Luther. "You!" he shrieked. "I killed ye once before, killed yer troublemakin' father. Now I'm goin' ta kill ya agin!"

He opened up with the pistol. Luther was caught out in the open. The range was considerable for a pistol, but Luther was forced to duck for cover. When he looked up again, Fife was gone. Luther could hear the sound of him running, heard boots splashing through puddles, heard Fife cursing and swearing.

Luther ran after him, careful now, worried about Fife popping out of a doorway as he passed by, peppering him with the pistol. But he made it all the way to the lift house, where he saw Fife duck inside a small doorway. Luther ran around the building to the main door. He poked his head around the corner cautiously, half-expecting a shot.

Fife was nowhere to be seen, but the lift equipment was running, the cage was on its way down the shaft. One more quick look around, then Luther ran over to the lift cage operator. "Where's Fife?" he demanded.

The operator, his eyes wide, stared at Luther's rifle. "He went down the hole," he finally answered. "He's in the cage."

"Well . . . stop the cage!" Luther snapped.

Swallowing hard, the lift operator reached out, pulled a lever. The cable stopped running out of its spool, jerked to a stop. "Bring it up," Luther demanded.

More work with the levers. The wire began to reel back onto its spool. Luther stood waiting, rifle ready, ready for his final confrontation with Duncan Fife.

He was distracted by movement near the door. He turned. Homer Jackson was entering the lift house, still carrying the shotgun. "You find him?" Homer asked.

"He's in the cage. On his way up."

"He telegraphed for the law, you know. I talked to the telegraph operator."

"It'll take them a day to get here."

The two men waited. Finally the cage was almost in view. Luther and Homer ducked behind some of the lift machinery, guns raised.

But there was no one in the cage; it was totally empty. Luther spun toward the lift operator. "Where the hell . . . ?"

The operator shrugged helplessly. "He musta got out. When I stopped the cage. He was right by a tunnel opening."

"Then send me down to the same level."

Homer seized him by the sleeve. "If you go down, he could be waiting right there, then shoot you like a trapped animal, before you can get out of the cage."

"I've gotta go down there."

"Wait, then."

Homer held a fast conversation with the lift operator, then came back to Luther. "Like I thought. The particular drift he's in, there's another just above it that slopes down, joins Fife's drift way back. You can go around the long way, then pin him against the main shaft, with no way out."

He gestured toward the lift operator with his shotgun. "I'll make sure this character don't play any funny games."

A moment later Luther was on his way down into the mine. It was as hot and sickening a trip as when he'd gone down that other time, so long ago. Only a boy then, on his way to deliver a message. Now he was on his way to deliver a bullet.

The cage jerked to a stop. Luther jumped out into the dimly lit opening of a tunnel. "Who's there?" he heard someone shout from below. It was Fife's voice.

Luther did not answer, ran deeper into the drift. There was a shift working, men looked up in surprise as he pressed on past them. The drift seemed to go on forever, but slanted down, always down. Finally, it debouched into another drift. If Homer was right, this was the drift where Fife had got out of the cage.

Luther moved along cautiously. Fife might be hidden anywhere along this dark, narrow passageway, ready to open fire. He doubted it; the men were still working. He walked up to a miner. "Have you seen Duncan Fife?"

The man spat out saliva mixed with drill dust. "Naw. But I heard him a while ago, caterwaulin' down by the main shaft."

So, Fife was still ahead of him. Luther started forward, found his way blocked by an ore car. Track had been laid inside the drift, to carry ore toward the main shaft. It was a very narrow drift; there was not much room on either side of the car.

"Hey," the miner said. "Don't I know you? I think I seen you around here a few years ago. A kid. . . ."

"Horace McCall's boy," Luther said grimly. He started to work his way around the ore car, but the man took him by the arm. "Hot damn!" he said excitedly. "So the bastards didn't kill you, after all." He was smiling. Now he stopped smiling. "I guess you come for Fife, huh?"

"Yeah."

Looking ahead, Luther could see all the way to the end of the drift, into the blackness of the main shaft beyond. There were bigger lamps at the mouth of the drift, lighting it well. He saw something move. A man. "Who the Divil's there?" he heard a voice call out, raw with fear.

"Luther McCall. I'm coming after you, Fife."

"No! You can't!" Followed by two shots. One bullet spanged off the ore car, the other hit the miner standing next to Luther in the arm. "Shit!" the miner grunted, grabbing his wounded arm. "That hurt like hell!"

Now Luther could hear the sound of a pistol hammer coming down on empty cylinders. "Oh God!" Fife shrieked. A moment later the empty pistol came flying out of the gloom, to clang off one of the tracks.

Now Fife's voice became wheedling. "I'm unarmed. Ya kin see that I've no weapon left. Ya can't shoot an unarmed man. If ye do, they'll hang ya so high . . ."

Luther silently cursed. The bastard was right, he couldn't shoot an unarmed man. Not even Fife. He just didn't have it in him.

The miner was not quite as picky. "Greedy, mean, nasty little bastard shot me in the arm," he snarled. "After slavin' my ass off in his mine for years, eatin' shit every day. . . . It's time somebody paid the son of a bitch back."

Before Luther knew what the miner was going to do, he'd released the brake on the ore car and pushed hard, sending it along the track. There was a slight downhill grade. The ore car picked up speed as it moved toward the mouth of the drift. Fife may have heard it coming, or perhaps not, because he was still babbling about being unarmed.

Now the ore car was almost on him, a mass of metal rumbling out of the darkness of the drift. Luther heard Fife cry out, "No!" a wild, despairing shout, then the car hammered through the first of the crash barriers, bent it aside, and slammed into Fife, knocking him out of the drift, into the main shaft.

The ore car was stopped short by the last crash barrier, bending it badly, but the car was still just inside the drift mouth. Luther could hear, faintly, Fife's scream as he fell down the shaft.

Luther and the miner ran to the mouth of the tunnel. The miner, clutching his wounded arm, looked over the edge. "Must not o' hit nothin' on the way down," he muttered. "I can still hear the bastard. He's in the sump."

Then Luther heard it too, a few last faint screams. Leaning out as far as he dared, he thought he saw something moving in the near-boiling water of the sump, far below, a last wild thrashing as Fife was scalded to death in the same pool where so many of his miners had met their own deaths.

Miner stew, Luther remembered. That's what that old miner had called the sump the day Luther had seen a man fall down the shaft.

He wondered how Fife liked the taste now.

Night had fallen by the time Luther was ready to ride out. Homer was standing in front of his shack, with the shotgun he'd taken from Tarkington leaning against the doorjamb. "The law'll be here by morning," he said glumly. "There's no way to cover up what happened . . . too many people seen it. They'll be after your hide, Luther. They'll never forget."

"Guess not," Luther replied. He felt curiously numb. It was over now, really all over. He'd settled his debts, he should be home free. But Homer was right. Those with power, those who feared the same kind of vengeance Luther had meted out to Duncan Fife, would not dare to forget what he had done. From now on, Luther's road would be lonely, dangerous, and probably very short.

He turned his horse's head, ready to ride away. Homer called out to him, "Was it worth it?"

Luther pulled back on the reins, surprised. Worth it? He'd never thought to ask himself that particular question. About the same as asking if breathing was worth it.

He looked down at Homer. "There are some things you just do," he said quietly.

Then he rode on out of the valley. Rode out into the immensity of the West.

SPECIAL PREVIEW!

If you liked DESPERADO, here's an exciting look at
book two of the adventures of Luther McCall, EDGE OF
THE LAW.

DESPERADO

On the razor's edge of the law,
one man walks alone . . .

The following is an excerpt from book two
in this action-packed Western series by B. W. Lawton,
available in July 1993 from Jove Books . . .

The rangy brown gelding between Luther McCall's knees sensed trouble a full minute before the rider did.

It showed in the quick flutter of nostrils as the horse snorted nervously and in the alert ears cocked toward the southwest. Luther felt the ripple of anticipation in the horse's wiry but powerful muscles.

Luther knew better than to ignore the signs. When it came to spotting danger, the brown gelding was a better watchdog than anyone's hound. A man who paid no attention to what his horse was trying to tell him didn't last long in this part of the West.

• After a moment, Luther dropped a hand to the horse's withers, a signal of reassurance. "Easy, Chili," he said softly, "I see it now." Luther's hand dropped to the stock of the Winchester rifle in its saddle scabbard as he squinted toward the faint smudge of smoke, flattened into a soft gray mist by the southwest wind. The smoke sifted from the mouth of a shallow valley beyond a rocky ridge in the broken hills north of the Cimarron River.

Smoke could mean several things, all of them trouble. Especially here in the place called the Cimarron Strip, a no-man's land populated by outlaws, an occasional band of bronco Indians who had bolted the reservation, or the nervous trigger fingers of wanderers who drifted into this stretch of wild country.

The tracks of the six men and the remuda of twenty stolen horses Luther followed were fresh, less than a day old. And the trail led straight toward the smoke. Luther damn well intended to catch up with the band, but on his own terms. That didn't include riding into the middle of a half dozen gunmen in broad daylight.

Luther couldn't have cared less about nineteen of the stolen horses; they belonged to a rich rancher with a pot belly back in Kansas, a man who built his fortune on other people's sweat. But the men up ahead had made one mistake.

One of the horses they had stolen belonged to Luther McCall.

Luther slipped the Winchester Model 73 from its scabbard, cracked the lever to make sure a cartridge was chambered and ready, then reined Chili toward a cluster of stunted junipers at the crest of the ridge. He pulled the brown to a stop just below the crest, swung down and made his way to the top. The wind-twisted evergreens gave him a good vantage point to check out the valley unobserved. He slid between two junipers, the oily scent of the trees heavy in his nostrils, and stared toward the valley below.

The remains of a settler's cabin lay a hundred yards away. Embers still winked in the charred logs. A slight shift of the wind brought a belly-wrenching scent to Luther's nostrils—the smell of burned human flesh. He pulled the Winchester hammer to full cock. There was no sign of movement, no hint of life, in the valley below.

Behind the smoldering logs that had been the cabin was a wrecked corral and a half-dugout that must have been used as a storage room or small barn. A jumbled woodpile lay halfway between the house and downed corral poles. A shallow, spring-fed creek bristling with wild berry vines twisted its way around the corral, flowed past the remnants of the cabin, and finally disappeared into a boggy seep beyond an overturned outhouse to the south. A pair of buzzards wheeled overhead. Luther doubted there would be much left for the scavengers after the fire died down.

He watched and waited for almost a half hour, saw nothing, and finally worked his way back down the ridge to his horse. "Damn fool nesters probably deserved whatever they got," Luther grumbled aloud. "No man with a lick of sense would settle in a God-forsaken place like this." He stepped into the saddle, sheathed the Winchester and kneed Chili into motion. He was about to circle the homestead and pick up the horse thieves' tracks on the other side when he decided to give the place a closer check. *Those buzzards up there might know something I don't,* he thought.

The stench of burned flesh was almost overpowering in what would have been the front yard of the cabin. Luther's nose wrinkled in revulsion at the scent. Chili didn't like it either. The brown snorted and danced sideways, skittish, as Luther urged the horse closer to the ruins. Luther didn't bother to dismount. There was nothing to see afoot that he couldn't see from horseback. Two charred, grotesquely twisted bodies lay in one corner of the cabin; if the dead settlers had possessed anything of value, it was long gone now, lining the pockets of a half-dozen horse thieves—

"Hold it right there, mister!"

Luther's right hand slapped against the butt of the Colt hung low on his right hip at unexpected sound. But something about the challenge stayed his hand; he didn't draw the weapon. The voice was thin, weak and high-pitched. The call came from the edge of the tangle of berry vines along the creek.

Luther turned toward the thicket and felt his eyebrows lift in surprise. A sandy-haired boy who couldn't be more than a dozen years old knelt at the edge of the thicket, his clothes smudged and tattered. Blood soaked the left shoulder of a tattered shirt. And he held a rifle, the small black hole in the muzzle wavering slightly but not straying far from Luther's chest. A .22-caliber bullet was bad news, Luther knew. Not because of its power, but because it made a dirty little hole. More men had died from infection caused by puny .22 slugs than from the heavy wallop of a .45.

"Son," Luther said casually, "you can get yourself dead pointing a gun at a man."

"And you can get just as dead if I pull this trigger." The boy's voice quavered, but the tone was serious. "You men took everything we had. Ain't nothing left to take. What did you come back for?"

"I had nothing to do with this. Just passing through and saw the smoke."

The boy squinted down the rifle barrel as if he were struggling to focus his eyes on the big man on the brown horse. The youth's face was almost stark white beneath the dirt and grime.

"I'll shoot if you move," the boy said. Under the weak and shaky words was a distinct note of determination. *The kid's got sand,* Luther thought. He slowly raised his hand from the butt of the Colt.

"What happened here, boy?"

"Some men came. They killed my Pa and my uncle. Shot me before I could use this rifle. I reckon they thought I was dead, too." The voice was rapidly growing weaker. "They burnt the house and stole our stock."

"Was one of the men big, like me? Wearing a duster and riding a black horse with a white star on his face?"

The rifle muzzle steadied on Luther's chest. "You know 'em, then?"

"Son, I've been tracking those horse thieves all the way from Kansas."

"You a lawman?"

Luther shook his head. "No. I'm just a man who wants to get his horse back." He stared toward the boy's bloody shirt. "Looks like you got hit pretty hard. You plan to stand there and bleed to death, or are you going to put that rifle down and let me help you?"

Indecision flickered in the boy's watery eyes. "How do I know you won't kill me?"

"You don't," Luther said, "and I like a man smart enough not to trust a stranger. For what it's worth, you have my word on it."

The youth's eyelids drooped. Luther could tell the lad was staying awake only by strength of will, and the boy had more of that than most grown men. After a moment the rifle muzzle wavered, then dropped.

"All right, mister. I reckon I'm likely to die anyway."

"Everyone does, eventually." Luther swung from the saddle and strode toward the boy, keeping most of his attention on the little .22 rifle bore. Luther McCall never took anything for granted. It was a good way to get dead. "The trick, son, is to put off that time as long as possible." He reached out, lifted the scarred Remington rolling-block single shot rifle from the youth's hand, and put the weapon carefully on the ground. "Now, let's take a look at that bullet hole." He pulled the bloody remnants of the boy's shirt back.

It was a nasty wound. A large-caliber bullet had hit the youth at an angle in the upper back, deflected off the shoulder blade and tore away a sizeable chunk of muscle when it came out at the top of his shoulder. The kid had to be hurting something fierce, Luther knew, but his eyes were still dry and the small, square jaw set in defiance of the pain. Luther was reasonably sure the slug hadn't cut any major blood vessels, or the boy would have been dead by now. But he had lost a hell of a lot of blood from a small frame.

"How—how bad is it?"

Luther sighed and shook his head. "Bad enough to worry about. We have to get that bleeding stopped right away." He stepped away for a moment, rummaged in a saddle bag, pulled out his one remaining clean shirt and a bottle of clear liquid. He lifted his canteen and returned to the youth's side. "This is going to hurt like old billy hell, son," Luther said, "but it's got to be done."

The boy ground his teeth against a fresh wave of pain, then nodded. "Couldn't hurt a lot more than it does now. Let's get it done."

Luther heard the air whistle through the boy's nostrils in a silent cry of agony as Luther dabbed the gore away from bullet-ravaged muscle. The boy didn't scream or even groan aloud. *Tough little guy,* Luther thought; *most grown men would be whimpering like babies by now.*

His admiration for the sandy-haired boy's courage grew as he worked on the wound. "You have a name, son?"

"Jimmy—Jimmy Macko." The words were slurred through clenched teeth.

"Well, Jimmy Macko, you're *hombre mucho,*" Luther said. "Much man." He finished cleaning the wound. The shoulder blade was probably cracked, if not broken, by the impact of the bullet, but the shoulder joint was intact. Luther struggled in sweaty silence for several minutes, dribbling raw alcohol onto torn flesh and swabbing it down. He heard the grind of small teeth against the blast of fiery pain from the disinfectant. Still, the boy remained awake. No tears streaked the dirty face.

Luther opened a small leather pouch at his belt, dribbled a mixture of herb leaves and ground tobacco onto the wound until the bleeding eased, then tore his clean shirt into sections. He bandaged the wound as best he could and tied the pad into place with strips ripped from the shirt sleeves. Finally, he stepped back and swiped a hand over his own sweaty forehead.

"That's about the best I can do for you out here, son," Luther said. "You need a doctor. Is there one around here?"

"Cim—Cimarron." The boy's voice was barely audible now, muted by pain, shock and loss of blood. He nodded toward the south. "Ain't much—of a town. No real doctor. But the marshal's wife's—nursed a lot of hurts."

Luther winced inwardly at the mention of the word marshal. He had no use for lawmen and good reasons for staying clear of them. He also found himself resenting the time he would lose in taking the boy into town. That would let the horse thieves gain a few more hours on him. He wasn't worried about losing the trail. Six men and twenty horses left a wide track, and by now he had a pretty good idea where they were headed.

What bothered Luther most was that he had been dealt a hand in a game he hadn't intended to play. The business on the homestead wasn't his affair. If the boy had been a man grown, Luther would have no qualms about mounting the brown and riding off to leave the wounded one to his own fate. But a kid—especially this particular kid—was a horse of a different breed. Luther McCall would never admit it, but he liked kids. If circumstances had been different, if he hadn't had a price on his head and every bounty hunter, lawman and would-be gunslinger in the West after his hair, he would have liked to have kids of his own. A man should leave something of himself behind when the sun went down for the last time.

He glanced at the boy. Jimmy's head nodded, the eyelids almost closed. He was fighting it hard, but he was on the thin edge of unconsciousness. One thing was for sure. Jimmy Macko, all twelve years worth, was a scrapper. Luther saw something of himself in the sandy-haired boy, a toughness that wouldn't let him cry from pain or loss.

"Mister?"

"Yes, Jimmy?"

"Pa—and Uncle Ed—"

"There's nothing we can do for them. They're gone. Maybe you can ask the marshal of this town to send somebody out to bury the—to bury them." Luther sighed. "We can't spare the time, son. We've got to get you some real help."

Luther gathered up the reins and led the snorting brown to the boy's side. "We'll have to ride double," he said, "and I'm not sure old Chili here is going to like that. He's twitchy at times."

"Chili—funny name—for a horse."

Luther almost smiled. "It fits. He's full of pepper and gives me a bellyache most of the time." Luther studied the brown and his rig. There wouldn't be much room for two riders, even if one of them wasn't a lot bigger than a mite. The single-fire saddle already carried two rifles—a Sharps Fifty for long range work and the Winchester for closer action—a bedroll, a possibles pack that held a few cooking utensils and a handful of food, and two saddle bags. The brown's eyes were wide, the whites showing all around, and the nostrils fluttered at the smell of blood.

Luther tied his canteen back onto the saddle and knelt beside the boy. "Might as well give it a try, Jimmy," he said. "Let's see how Chili feels about it."

He helped the boy to his feet and, talking softly to the snorting, walleyed brown, eased Jimmy into the saddle. Chili shied a bit, stomped his feet and tossed his head, then settled down under

Luther's firm hand. Luther toed the stirrup.

"Mister?" Jimmy's voice was strained and growing fainter under the renewed agony of movement in mounting the horse.

"Yes?"

"My—rifle. Don't forget—rifle."

Luther stooped, retrieved the little Remington, checked the action—there was a live round in the chamber—and lowered the hammer. "What do you need it for?"

"To—to kill those—men some day. For what they—what they did here."

Luther slipped the short rifle beneath the straps of his bedroll. "Can't think of a better reason to keep it around, Jimmy," he said. "Now, let's get into town. Before you pass out on me, tell me which way to ride."

The boy described a few prominent landmarks as Luther mounted and settled himself in the saddle, careful not to jostle Jimmy more than necessary. "Plain enough, Jimmy," he said as he reined the antsy brown toward the south. "Let's go find Cimarron."

J.R. ROBERTS

THE

GUNSMITH